MYSTERIES *of* MARTHA'S VINEYARD

A Light in the Darkness
Like a Fish Out of Water
Adrift
Maiden of the Mist
Making Waves

MYSTERIES *of* MARTHA'S VINEYARD

Making Waves

TRICIA GOYER & CARA PUTMAN

Guideposts

New York

Mysteries of Martha's Vineyard is a trademark of Guideposts.

Published by Guideposts Books & Inspirational Media
110 William Street
New York, NY 10038
Guideposts.org

This is a work of fiction. Martha's Vineyard, Massachusetts, actually exists, and some
characters are based on actual residents whose identities have been fictionalized to
protect their privacy. Apart from the actual people, events, and locales that figure into
the fiction narrative, all other names, characters, businesses, and events are the creation
of the authors' imaginations or are used fictitiously.

Every attempt has been made to credit the sources of copyrighted material used in this
book. If any such acknowledgment has been inadvertently omitted or miscredited,
receipt of such information would be appreciated.

Scripture references are from the following sources: The Holy Bible, King James
Version (KJV). Scripture quotations marked (NIV) are taken from *The Holy Bible,
New International Version*. Copyright ©1973, 1978, 1984, 2011 by Biblica, Inc.
Used by permission of Zondervan. All rights reserved worldwide. www.zondervan.com

Cover and interior design by Müllerhaus
Cover illustration by Greg Copeland, represented by Deborah Wolfe, LTD.
Typeset by Aptara, Inc.

Printed and bound in the United States of America
10 9 8 7 6 5 4 3 2 1

Making Waves

CHAPTER ONE

A salty breeze wafted through Priscilla's open car window as she drove through the storybook village of Vineyard Haven. It was warmer today than it had been the last couple of weeks. November had blown in with a chilling fury, and Priscilla was thankful for the sun and the respite from the frigid temperatures. November had also brought sad memories: grief over Gary's death, thoughts of their last anniversary, and even further-back memories of her last visit to Martha's Vineyard with her mother. That last Thanksgiving, when she was only eight years old, had brought about a dispute that had kept her from the island for fifty years—a feud between her mother and aunt that she didn't completely understand, but at which time had chipped away, like the waves against a rocky outcropping.

Trying to push those gray thoughts from her mind, Priscilla hummed "Boogie Woogie Bugle Boy" and waved her finger to the beat as she pulled up in front of the East Shore Historical Museum. With a smile she parked, rolled up her window, and then got out and moved to the other side of the car to grab the bags of paper goods she had set on the passenger seat. She pushed the passenger door shut with her foot and then shifted her bags as she walked up the sidewalk to the small museum.

When Mildred Pearson had asked for help setting up for the hundredth birthday celebration for one of the town's special citizens, Priscilla had quickly agreed. It felt good to know her friend was willing to ask her for help, and Priscilla looked forward to meeting the honored guest.

The Martha's Vineyard residents considered Deanie Spangler, a World War II veteran, something of a local hero after she received the Congressional Gold Medal seven years ago. Now it was time to honor this woman with a party to celebrate her milestone birthday. To get in the mood Priscilla had listened to classic songs from World War II, and the catchy melodies wouldn't leave her thoughts. *He had a boogie style that no one else could play...* Her finger continued to shake as she moved to the building, and it amazed her that Deanie actually had played an important part in the history she'd only read about.

The museum building was a sunny yellow Queen Anne Victorian tucked slightly off the road. Priscilla smiled as she noted the small Happy Birthday banner that ruffled in the breeze from its post at the top of the porch. She climbed the wide, pale gray steps and crossed the old-fashioned porch to the front door of the converted house. She shifted the bags again so she could twist the knob and open the door.

The moment she entered, she saw Mildred wore her gray hair up in its normal twist and was dressed in a pair of navy slacks paired with a cashmere sweater set in a lovely coral. Mildred was one of the few women who could make Priscilla feel petite. "There you are. I was beginning to worry."

Priscilla held up the bags. "I got everything you asked for." She glanced at her watch. "And I'm not even a minute later than I told you I'd arrive." Mildred was such a stickler for punctuality. Priscilla had learned to arrive a few minutes early to any appointment with her friend. She entered the museum then turned to Mildred. "You look nice."

"Once in a while it's appropriate not to wear period clothes." Mildred turned and walked briskly toward the reception area. "I have several tables set up over here. I also have a few chairs, but we need to organize them. Deanie will need a chair, and we'll want to have a few rows for her friends."

"How about setting them up as conversation groups? There's not a formal program, is there?"

"No, it's supposed to be informal, so we can try groups as long as they fit in the space."

Priscilla set the bags on the table Mildred indicated and then started pulling out the tablecloths. It only took a moment to cover the tables. Then the women worked together to arrange the plates, cups, and utensils on the tables.

Mildred indicated the first table. "We'll have the cake and punch bowl there. Then that table will have the basket for cards and any gifts people bring."

Priscilla nodded as she scattered fall-colored confetti of reds, oranges, and yellows across the table. "It'll be nice."

"I hope so." Mildred sighed and cocked a hip against a table. "Deanie's family has been part of our community for generations.

She's earned an evening of celebration, but the family insisted on keeping it small."

"I imagine many of her friends are gone."

"True." Mildred stepped from the table and headed to the small kitchen. "Did I tell you she's donating her Congressional Gold Medal as well as her WASP uniform and paraphernalia to the museum? We're going to set up a permanent display."

"That's exciting. Why did she receive the medal again?"

"Here, let me show you." Mildred set a pitcher of water on the food table then led Priscilla to a display table Priscilla hadn't noticed. "She received the award for her years of service as a Woman Airforce Service Pilot. Until she was honored in 2010, many of us didn't know she'd served as a WASP."

"She was a pilot?"

Mildred nodded. "I've heard that Deanie's first flights before the war were shuttle flights from the mainland to the island and taking the occasional visitor up for an aerial tour. Then a letter showed up inviting her to apply for a new division of female pilots. I guess it was hard back then to find enough people with the required minimum flight hours, so they started asking women."

"I've always thought that would have been a fascinating way to serve."

"You'd never know all that she's accomplished by talking to Deanie, but I agree. She downplays that she did anything special, but I think that's a characteristic of her generation." Mildred slipped off a velvet cloth covering the display case. Inside was a shelf with a letter that looked like the invitation to apply for the special group. Next to it was a scrapbook and below that a uniform and hat were arranged. And next to the uniform and hat was a shining, gold medal. It was larger than a silver dollar and featured an image of a WASP with three pilots in the foreground in flight uniforms walking toward their aircraft. Tears pricked Priscilla's eyes. The display represented a woman's life, a woman's sacrifice, and finally, a woman's honor.

"The other side of the medal features the three types of aircraft flown by the WASPs: trainers, fighters, and bombers. Deanie told me specifically which types of aircraft they were, but I've forgotten. I'm sure she'll tell you if you ask." Mildred tilted her head and looked at the display case with pride. "I have a special tray for the medal. The case is designed to let us slip everything easily from the back. Deanie wanted those attending tonight to have the opportunity to see it up close."

Priscilla ran her fingers along the edge of the display. Her father-in-law, Clifford, had been a World War II veteran, but he never wanted to talk about it. Gary had told her that his dad had experienced many painful things and that talking about them was reliving them. "That's exciting she's willing to share her medal with everyone like that. What a true gift."

"Yes." Mildred winked. "You'll have to ask her about how she received it. And who she received it from."

Priscilla smiled, knowing it wouldn't be hard to have a conversation with Deanie, especially since she'd been honored by congressional leaders. Priscilla had so many questions about what Deanie had done and seen during the war.

Mildred glanced at her watch. "The guests will start arriving anytime. Will you watch the table for me during the party? I don't want anyone sticking their fingers in the cake or getting too close to the medal." Mildred cocked an eyebrow. "They can look, but let's make sure they don't touch."

"Absolutely." Priscilla took another look at the display then settled the velvet cloth back in place. "Anything else you need me to do right now?"

"Just click on the music. I've got a Glenn Miller CD ready to go. I figured that will be something Deanie will enjoy. Then if you could check out front and see if our guest of honor has arrived, I'd appreciate it."

"Sure." Priscilla stopped near the desk and turned on the music. Soon the strains of big-band tunes filled the space, and she headed toward the front windows. Her eyes widened as she looked out.

"Mildred," she called. "Are you sure it's a secret? Because something's got the attention of the town." Several cars had joined hers, and others were pulling into the lot. "How many people did you say we expected?" All down the main street there seemed to be a long line of arriving vehicles.

They aren't all coming here, are they?

"Twenty or thirty guests."

"I think you need to revise that number." Priscilla did a quick count as people exited their cars. She recognized the guest of honor immediately. An older woman with tight white curls and wearing pink was being helped from a car into a wheelchair. "It looks like

Deanie's here, and from what I can see of the people parking, we've already exceeded thirty people—and more cars are arriving."

"Oh my." Mildred hurried to the window and stood next to Priscilla. Her mouth dropped open when she saw the full parking lot with people streaming in from all directions.

Priscilla also noticed a man with a camera hanging around his neck and a notebook in hand. Had the media arrived?

"Oh dear. Even the newspaper is here," Mildred mumbled under her breath, confirming Priscilla's guess. "The family wanted it to be a small event."

Priscilla placed a hand to her cheek. "Who else knew?"

"I don't know. I said something about it to Jedd Patterson, the local reporter who's making his way inside. I asked him to mention the new display in an article next week, but I made sure he knew today's birthday celebration was a private event." Mildred sighed. "I specifically told him not to let the word out yet. The last thing I wanted was to overwhelm Deanie with a large crowd—she is one hundred years old, after all."

"Maybe we can send away the uninvited guests?" Priscilla watched as the first group came toward the door.

"Good idea." Mildred stepped outside, with Priscilla right behind her, and raised her hands. "I'm sorry. Did you each receive an invitation to this event? It's a private, family affair."

A tall man with salt-and-pepper hair shook his head. "That's not what I heard."

"Me either," said the stocky woman next to him.

"I'm sorry there's been a miscommunication, but I really must insist you leave." Mildred took advantage of every inch of height she had, but a warbling voice halted whatever else she planned to say.

Joan Abernathy, Priscilla's cousin, slowed where she was on the sidewalk. "Are you sure? There are so many of us here to celebrate our lovely lady. Deanie is considered a sweet friend by many on the island."

"I really must insist." Mildred stiffened her posture, and Priscilla imagined she was ready to defend the right and wrong of the party.

Just then a tall young man worked his way up the sidewalk, pushing Deanie in a wheelchair. His jacket was exquisitely tailored and layered over a cable wool sweater, the perfect relaxed yet formal Martha's Vineyard fall look. Add in his loafers and pressed khakis, and he looked stiff next to the hot pink bling that Deanie wore.

"Are all these people here for me? How wonderful!" Deanie Spangler was a sparrow of a woman as she sat in the wheelchair. Her posture was still straight, but her skin was fragile as tracing paper stretching across slim limbs. Her blue eyes sparkled beneath her cap of snow-white hair. "I love a good party."

Priscilla glanced at the man pushing the wheelchair. "Would you like everyone to stay?"

The woman of honor nodded before the younger man could say a word. "I've always loved a big celebration. The more the merrier! I've attended some amazing shindigs during my time, but rarely was the party for me." She clapped her hands with delight.

Her smile lit her face from within, stretching the hot pink lipstick where it had slid into the wrinkles around her mouth.

Mildred looked around. "Well then, let's have them stay." She placed a hand on Priscilla's arm as she leaned toward her. "Even though it's warmer today, too bad it's still too cold to keep the party outside." She sighed as she glanced toward the kitchen. "And pray we have enough cake and punch. Maybe not everyone will want some."

The crowd of people continued to stream through the door. They chatted with each other, but one voice rose above them all.

"Let's get me out of this wheelchair and to a place where I can enjoy everyone." Deanie's words were stated with a regal air, but Priscilla noted the fun behind them.

Priscilla nodded toward the door. "Maybe we could station you near the door but away from the cold air. Then you could say hello to everyone as they arrive."

"That's perfect, dear." Deanie turned to the man pushing her. "Andrew, I'd like that to happen."

"All right, Aunt Deanie, but I think you might be more comfortable if you stayed in the chair."

"Shows how rarely you've ridden in one of these contraptions!" Deanie reached up and patted his hand. "You take good care of me, Andy, but I insist. I will not spend the evening in this chair."

Mildred leaned close to Priscilla's ear. "That's her great-nephew, Andrew Wright. Deanie doesn't have any children, but thankfully Andrew has always been there for her. He lives near the retirement home where she lives and helped plan the party." Then, offering a smile that Priscilla knew was forced, Mildred turned to the pair.

"Then let's get you settled. And oh, what a lovely surprise all these extra guests are!"

With commanding steps, Mildred guided Andrew to park the wheelchair in a corner near the parlor entrance. Together they helped Deanie toward a more comfortable padded chair that Priscilla brought out from the elegant parlor. Once Deanie was settled, Mildred turned back to Priscilla. "If you could stay near Deanie and also try to keep an eye on the display table, I'd appreciate it. I'm going to see if I can figure out how to cut the cake to make it go further."

"Sure." Priscilla wouldn't mind the chance to talk with Deanie, but it only took minutes before the elderly woman was surrounded by well-wishers. She slipped away every few minutes to check the table and then eased back to see if the guest of honor needed anything.

Deanie allowed each well-wisher to shake her bird-like hands or kiss her wrinkled cheeks. Delight brightened her eyes as person after person wished her a happy birthday and conversed with her. Most of the visitors were from town, and they made it clear Deanie was well-loved. Others seemed to have heard about the event as they'd enjoyed their stay—visitors who'd come to Martha's Vineyard to catch the last days of the brilliant fall colors. They mostly wanted to see what the fuss was about but were delighted to be introduced to a woman who played such an important part in United States history.

Mildred stepped in front of her desk and clapped her hands. Priscilla gave a shrill whistle, and the voices stilled. "Thank you to everyone for coming." Mildred smiled at the assemblage. "It's a delight to have you here as we honor Deanie Spangler."

Priscilla slipped into the small kitchen to get the lighter. She lit the ten candles clustered around Deanie's name on the large sheet cake.

Deanie clapped her hands in delight. "Is all that for me?"

"Let's sing 'Happy Birthday,' and then our guest of honor can make a wish," Mildred instructed.

"And blow out the candles." Deanie tittered as she edged closer, her great-nephew keeping a close eye on her, looking ready to launch forward to grab her if needed.

Priscilla stepped toward her. "Let me help you."

A moment later as everyone sang the classic birthday song, Deanie stood, leaning on Priscilla and Andrew, her grin revealing perfect dentures. As soon as the song ended, she shuffled to the table and then blew out the candles in two attempts. Everyone applauded, and she took a small bow before sitting again.

Mildred waved for the crowd's attention. "Feel free to get some cake and punch and continue to say hello to Deanie. After a bit we'll unveil a surprise."

People strolled by the still-covered display case without slowing, eager to get their cake and punch. As the sugary drink disappeared, Priscilla filled the bowl with more. She kept an eye on the supplies and nibbled her bottom lip as she wondered if the cake and punch would last for everyone. One by one people stopped to say a word with Deanie and then took their places in the refreshment line.

Instead of overwhelming her, the crowd imparted energy to Deanie. The longer they chatted, the more she perked up and glowed. Finally, thirty minutes later than planned, Mildred regained the crowd's attention. Andrew had wandered off from his great-aunt, and Priscilla tried to keep a closer eye on Deanie.

"It's time for a presentation the museum is thrilled about." Mildred stepped through the crowd and stopped in front of the covered display.

"And it's one I'm delighted to make." Deanie gestured toward Priscilla. "Will you help me stand?"

"Of course." After Deanie stood, Priscilla helped her to the display case, still looking for Andrew. He was nowhere to be seen.

Mildred beamed at the centenarian. "Please remove the cloth."

Deanie grinned. "With pleasure." She tugged off the velvet cover. Then her eyes widened, and she gasped and clutched her chest. The color drained from the older woman's face, and Priscilla wrapped her arms around Deanie's waist as her knees gave out. It took every ounce of strength Priscilla had to keep Deanie from tumbling to the floor.

CHAPTER TWO

After easing Deanie into her wheelchair, Priscilla blinked and tried to clear her vision. There must be some mistake. The medal had been nestled in place when Mildred had shown it to her not an hour and a half earlier. Now as she stared at the display case, she saw that the gold medal with the plane and women on the front was gone.

Deanie leaned forward and sagged against the display. "Where's my medal?"

Priscilla stepped closer. "Maybe it slid off its little pillow." Yet even as she drew nearer, she knew that was unlikely. A closer look confirmed her fear. The slim disc was not inside the case.

How could someone have slipped the medal out without anyone seeing?

The museum was filled with people. But maybe that was exactly how it had happened. There had been so much chatter and excitement focused on Deanie, it would have been relatively easy to open the access panel at the back and slip the medal out. The medal was small enough that someone could have tucked it into a pocket or purse without any effort.

Mildred's face was almost as pale as Deanie's. "Someone call the police!"

A buzz rose from the crowd.

Andrew appeared, striding toward them. "What happened?"

"The Congressional Gold Medal isn't here." Priscilla kept her voice low, hoping to keep him from reacting like his great-aunt. "It—it's gone..."

"How could you let that happen? I only stepped away for a few minutes." He spat out the words, and then he turned to Deanie. "We'll get the medal back, Aunt. Don't you worry about that." He cocked an eyebrow and narrowed his gaze on Mildred. Unspoken threats of *or else* hung in the air. Then with a flourish, he whipped out a large smartphone and pressed a few buttons. He stepped out of earshot, moving with quickened steps to the kitchen.

"Who would take the medal?" The quiver in the guest of honor's voice made Priscilla wish she could pull the medal out of a crack. "It's such a special award, but limited to people who served in a special way. Not everyone would care about it. It doesn't make sense for someone to take it."

"It must be here somewhere. We'll find it." Priscilla patted Deanie's arm and then stepped away toward the gathered townspeople. "Has anyone seen a gold medal? It's about this size." She formed a small circle with her fingers. "It has women and planes on it."

Murmurs rose from the crowd, but no one stepped forward. She bit her lower lip and let her gaze move from face to face. They all wore confused or surprised looks. No one appeared to be hiding anything. Besides, if someone had taken it, they wouldn't simply step forward. Hopefully the police would be able to locate it with a few interviews and a search. They knew better what to do in such a situation.

Priscilla pressed a firm hand against her stomach, trying to still the unsettled feeling. She was supposed to watch the display, but she couldn't do that and help the guest of honor too. *I should have found someone to help. I'm sure Joan wouldn't have minded lending a hand.*

Of course, hindsight was 20/20. The fact was, neither she nor Mildred had done what was necessary to protect the medal. Mildred had run back and forth as much as she had. That left plenty of time when the display stood unguarded and unwatched. It would have been relatively easy for someone who knew what was to be unveiled to step behind the display and slide the door open just long enough to slip the medal out. With its compact size, it would have been simple to scoop it away.

Andrew returned from the kitchen. "The police are on their way. The dispatcher said no one should leave before they arrive."

Mildred nodded then cleared her throat. She lifted her arms in the air, beckoning everyone's attention. "All right. The police are coming to help us locate the medal. Please stay where you are until they arrive. Thank you."

Hugh Latham, her cousin Gail's father, stepped around a middle-aged woman and approached Deanie. Hugh was almost as round as he was tall, the result of his passion for hummingbird cake. He scratched his balding scalp as he leaned toward the woman. "You all right, Dee?"

"I don't know." The woman's fingers fluttered to her throat. "Why would anyone take the medal? It means so much to me. The years it took for the government to finally acknowledge all that my friends and I did during the war." Tears filled her eyes. "I only wanted to share it with our town. My service is part of *our* history. Vineyard Haven's history."

He nodded and cleared his throat. "You did a good thing there, trying to share your honor with our town." Then Uncle Hugh jutted out his chin as he turned to Priscilla. "You need help looking for it?"

Priscilla blinked against the moisture filling her eyes, noting his kindness. "Yes. Feel free to look around the display case. Maybe I missed something." She wished it were as simple as her overlooking the flash of metal, but Priscilla had a sinking feeling in the pit of her gut that told her it was more than that.

Hugh shuffled around to the back and took his time looking in the display case. While he examined the display, Priscilla again scanned the crowd. She recognized some of the people in the museum, yet there were still many she didn't recognize. While Martha's Vineyard was feeling more like home each day, it reminded her she was still a relative newcomer to the island. As she caught sight of Ida Lee Jones and Candy Lane, she felt pride in the sense of community that had developed for her while she was here.

Only minutes passed when red-and-blue lights flashed through the windows, drawing her attention. A minute later Officer Ed Sequeira entered then stilled as he saw the people crowded into the building. "Well, hello all."

Mildred hurried up to him, her flats clicking against the floor. "I'm so glad you're here. We need your help."

"So I heard." He put his hands on his belt. "What happened?"

"Deanie Spangler donated some of her items from World War II, and we had planned to unveil them tonight at her hundredth birthday party."

"From my time as a WASP," Deanie piped up.

"All right." He pulled out a notebook and jotted a note. "And why am I here?"

Priscilla gestured toward the display case where the velvet cover lay along the side. "The Congressional Gold Medal disappeared. Someone must have taken it, because it was there before the party."

He glanced around the full room. "I'm going to need some help." He cleared his throat and then spoke with authority. "Folks, I'll need you to stay in place. I'm going to get some help, and we'll get you out of here just as soon as we can." He nodded toward Deanie and then stepped into the kitchen and pulled out his radio.

Priscilla looked around at the people filling the 1812 parlor and 1850s dining room. She could also see a few of the folks crowded into the 1790s pantry. "What should we do with everyone to keep them entertained?"

Deanie nodded off a bit in her chair as if drained by the excitement and adrenaline. Andrew stepped behind her. "I really should get her home—to Vineyard Village. It's been too much for her."

"If she weren't so worn out, I'd suggest she share stories of her experience." Mildred sighed. "What a terrible conclusion to an event that was supposed to focus on her."

"Definitely not the way I envisioned things when we talked." Andrew leaned down and lightly touched his great-aunt's shoulder. "Aunt Deanie? I think I should get you back to your room."

The small woman snapped awake, and her eyes looked extra large behind her glasses. "What?"

"Ready to go home?"

"Not yet, young man. Always so eager to get to the next thing." The woman tried to straighten but groaned. "Do you think you can get me a drink of water before we go?" Andrew nodded and moved through the assembled guests. Watching him go, Deanie turned to Priscilla. "You may not believe this, young lady, but I'm not afraid to die."

Priscilla startled at the quick change of topic. She tried to deflect Deanie. "I don't know that anyone's called me a young lady in at least thirty years. Life on the farm was good, but it was hard work." Priscilla stretched her back for emphasis, noting the years of strain.

"When you get to be my age, everyone's younger." The frail woman sighed. "It's not that I fear dying. At my age, so many of my friends have passed before me. Life can be lonely. That's what's made tonight so grand."

"It has been fun." Absent the missing medal.

"What I really wanted was to share my experience with others. I don't want what my friends and I accomplished in the war to be lost to time. That's why I've donated these items. They're precious to me, but the story belongs to everyone." She sighed. "I'm not afraid to die. I trust in the good Lord, after all. My hope is a bit of my story will be passed on. I hope my lasting legacy won't be that I lost what I waited so long to claim—that some thief robbed me of living on in this community after I'm gone."

Priscilla took Deanie's thin hand in her own. She gently squeezed it and caressed the soft, gentle skin with her thumb. "What you did in the past is important. So important it mustn't be forgotten. I promise, Deanie, I'll do all I can to see that the medal is returned."

A glimmer of hope brightened the woman's eyes, and as she turned her attention to her approaching great-nephew, Priscilla released her grip.

Andrew handed Deanie a plastic cup filled with water. "Here you go, Aunt. And we should get going. I'm afraid staying will be too much of a strain on you."

Deanie patted his hand and straightened her shoulders. Then she looked Priscilla in the eyes. "Promise me again that you will help find the medal."

Priscilla knew she shouldn't make such promises, but how could she say no to a hero like Deanie? "Yes, I'll do all I can."

Deanie's gaze was focused and intense. She breathed in a deep breath, seeming to take on a strength that had been absent minutes before. "Make sure you do." Her words pierced Priscilla, making her feel like the loss of the medal was her responsibility.

"Aunt Deanie, we should go. They'll be wondering where you are at Vineyard Village. I didn't think we'd be gone this late."

Priscilla placed her hand on his arm. "Let me make sure it's okay for you to leave. It'll only take a minute to check with Officer Sequeira."

"Another five minutes won't harm a thing." Deanie grinned, but it was strained. "I'm tougher than most think I am."

Priscilla tried to make her way to the kitchen quickly, but with the crowd pressing in, everything seemed to slow.

Officer Sequeira was reattaching his radio when she walked in. "Everything okay, ma'am?"

While Deanie calling her a young lady had been unsettling, she really didn't like "ma'am" much better. "Andrew Wright wants to take his great-aunt home."

"She is?"

"The guest of honor, Deanie Spangler."

"The woman whose medal is missing?"

"Yes."

"That should be all right. I can talk with her later."

"I'll let them know." As she helped Andrew get the chair through the crowd, seeing the shadow of sadness on Deanie's face where there'd only been delight before, Priscilla determined she would do all she could to recover the medal.

A hero such as Deanie deserved no less.

CHAPTER THREE

Andrew pushed Deanie Spangler from her party, and low murmurs filled the small museum. The crowd was getting restless. Priscilla could feel their frustration rising as no one explained what had happened. She overheard muffled conversations. People talking about the strange something that kept them constrained to the museum. What could have disappeared that was so important they couldn't leave?

What should have been a light, festive celebration was quickly heading south. People muttered among themselves, and Priscilla wouldn't be surprised to see people slip away—something that couldn't happen if one of those individuals had pocketed the medal.

Someone in this space had taken the medal. There were no other options. The medal had been there when Mildred originally showed her the display.

She turned to Mildred. "I'm going to wait by the doors. Try to keep people from leaving before Officer Sequeira is ready."

"That's a good idea." Mildred sighed. Her shoulders slumped beneath her sweater set. "I still can't believe this happened."

"No one but you and Jedd Patterson knew about the donation?"

"Add in Deanie, and we're the only ones who knew." Mildred glanced around the museum. "I've known these people for years, Priscilla. I know you're just starting to know them, but I can't imagine any of them stealing something like this. We were all so pleased for Deanie when she and her fellow WASPs received the recognition. Even if someone else knew, I can't imagine who would take the medal."

Priscilla patted Mildred's arm. "We'll find it."

Officers April Brown and Teddy Holmes arrived and headed straight to Officer Sequeira. "What do you need, Ed?" April was no-nonsense as she studied him with her hands on her utility belt.

"We need to interview all these people. Collect names, contact information, and what they saw." He pointed to the display case. "Mrs. Spangler's Congressional Gold Medal disappeared some-time during the event."

Officer Brown nodded and surveyed the museum. "Let's each take a room. We can make sure we interview everyone that way." She glanced around the rooms. "I'll take the parlor. Let's get these folks out of here quickly."

Officer Sequeira nodded. "Sounds good. Holmes, you can take the dining room." He stepped forward and got everyone's attention. "If some of you could go into the parlor, some into the kitchen, and some stay here in the foyer, we will do our best to interview you promptly so you can leave in a timely fashion. Thank you."

The officers split up, and Priscilla walked to the door quietly, reminding people they needed to enter one of the rooms and stay awhile longer. "The officers are collecting information now. It won't be long, and you'll be free to go."

As she stood at the door, Priscilla looked for Jedd Patterson, the reporter. She hadn't seen him in a while, but if he was still there, she wanted to talk to him. Was it possible he had mentioned the medal to someone? If he had, that person could have mentioned it to another. Then it could have passed on like a small-town version of the telephone game.

Her cousin Gail approached her, a worried crease adding to the wrinkles that layered character on her face. Her bobbed brown hair curled around her face, and only the lightest strokes of makeup set off her pretty gray-blue eyes. "Do you think they'll find the medal?"

"They have a good chance." Though secretly Priscilla worried how many had slipped away from the crowd before they noticed the missing medal. "Can you think of anyone who was here but is already gone?"

Gail considered the question a moment. "Not off the top of my head, but I can ask around."

"That would be great." Priscilla also knew she needed to ask Deanie if she'd told anyone about the medal. It was common knowledge she'd received it, but would she have told people she was donating it or would she have waited to make a big splash with a surprise?

The medal was special for the sentimental reasons attached to it. It had been given to the WASPs by the leaders of Congress, but

Priscilla was fairly certain it didn't have much actual value. That was something she could check on though.

Movement caught her attention, and Priscilla followed it until she recognized Jedd. Good, he hadn't left yet. Instead, he was moving from door to door, making notes about something before moving to another room and back again. With the police force of the small community here interviewing people, it made sense that this was where news would occur.

The minutes ticked by as the police systematically talked to those at the museum. They also checked everyone's purses, pockets, and bags. As she watched from her self-appointed post at the front door, Priscilla was pleased to see how deliberate they were about talking to each person. They didn't appear rushed, yet they were making steady progress through the eighty or so people in the museum. It sounded like the questions were straightforward: name, address, phone number, where were you? Then on to the next person. One by one she watched people move into the entryway.

The officers congregated in the kitchen after an hour.

Officer Holmes straightened his back. "I got everyone in my room."

"Me too." Officer Brown slipped her notebook into a pocket. "I didn't learn much."

"Not much to report from my room either. I think we can let everyone go."

Mildred hustled up, her strides as long as her face. "Did you find it?"

"No, ma'am." Officer Sequeira stepped back, making space. "We'll follow up and let you know if there's anything else we need."

"Don't you want to collect evidence before you leave?" Joan sounded disappointed as she inserted herself in the conversation.

Officer Sequeira looked like he couldn't decide whether to humor her or run. "What did you have in mind?"

Joan leaned toward him as if her small frame could compel him to act the way she wanted. In her brown tweed pants and beige turtleneck she resembled a sparrow, curiosity focused on him. "I'd think you wouldn't want to run the risk of missing important evidence, like who left this cup here."

"What?" Officer Brown looked as puzzled as she sounded.

Joan pointed to a Styrofoam cup abandoned on the display table. Dark purple lipstick edged it where someone had taken a drink. "Shouldn't you put that in a baggie? Take it to the station to see whose lipstick is on it?"

Officer Holmes chuckled. "This is Vineyard Haven, not *CSI: New York*."

"Sure." Joan frowned at him, reminding Priscilla she was used to keeping young men in line since she'd had practice with her two. "You should take this seriously, Officer."

"We are." He turned away from her back to Mildred. "Ma'am, if you think of anything else, let us know. Otherwise, we'll go talk with Mrs. Spangler. See what she can add to the investigation."

"Thank you." Mildred's smile was firm, yet trembled at the edges. The evening's events had shaken her, not surprising since the museum was such an important part of her life.

As Priscilla watched their interaction, questions pricked her mind.

Would the police take this disappearance seriously, or did they think that by showing up and conducting quick interviews with those in attendance, they'd done all that could be expected? Did they understand the significance of the medal?

Deanie had left before they could talk to her, so maybe they didn't truly understand.

As the officers left, the remaining party guests edged toward the door. Priscilla stepped in front of them and held up a hand. "Thank you, everyone, for staying. If you saw the medal or know anything about its whereabouts, please let the police or Mildred know. Deanie is crushed at its disappearance. It would be a wonderful birthday gift to her to get it back in the display case so she can share it with all of us." She stepped from the doorway and watched as the crowd disbanded.

Individuals flowed through the door alone or in small groups, making their way to the parking lot and then their cars. Joan and Gail offered to stay and help with cleanup, but Mildred encouraged them to head home. "Thanks for offering, but Priscilla and I can handle it."

Priscilla glanced around, noting the full trash cans and tracks where people had walked through cake crumbs. Yet one glance at Mildred's face was all she needed to know that the last thing her friend desired was more company. She hugged Gail and then leaned down to hug Joan. "Thanks for the offer."

Her cousins nodded then walked out together.

Priscilla turned back to Mildred. "How can I best help?"

"Find the medal?" Mildred laughed, but it was a broken sound. "I can't believe this happened."

Priscilla squeezed Mildred's arm. "We'll keep our eyes open as we clean. Maybe we'll find it in a crevice or nook we couldn't see with everyone here."

Mildred nodded then went to the janitor's small closet and pulled out a broom. "If you'll sweep, I'll start gathering the trash. Then we can tackle the individual rooms."

The women worked quietly, and over the next hour the museum came back to order. Yet no matter how carefully she looked, Priscilla didn't see the medal. As the women finished tearing down the food table, she sighed. "I really thought we'd find the medal."

"I'm afraid that's a foolish hope." Mildred placed her hands on her hips as she surveyed the museum. "Things are as good as they're going to get for now. We should go home. Either the police will find the one who has it, or we'll see things through fresh eyes tomorrow. Staying here looking everywhere we've already checked isn't going to solve a thing."

Priscilla wanted to argue with Mildred, remembering clearly the distress on Deanie Spangler's face. That medal meant much more to her than a simple award. It represented the efforts she and her friends had made that had gone largely unrecognized for years. Priscilla vowed she would do all in her power to help return the medal to its owner.

But what could she do on her own? Where could she look? If only she knew the answers to those questions. If only she knew where to start.

CHAPTER FOUR

The next morning Priscilla awoke unsettled after a restless night's sleep. She'd woken early, and Jake, her young stray that looked like he had Australian shepherd in him, took that as a sign she was as eager for a walk as he was. If he had his way, they'd spend each morning walking the beach, no matter how brisk the air.

"All right, Jake. We'll go." Maybe the air would invigorate her and clear her mind. Her dreams had been muddled, influenced by the prior night's affairs. Somehow she felt responsible for the loss of the medal, even though she knew there wasn't a thing she could have done. Not with so many people attending the birthday celebration.

Jake tugged at his leash where it hung on a peg next to the door, and she laughed. The boy was insistent they would go for a stroll. She bundled up against the oncoming chill, but even so shuddered as she opened the front door.

The moment the door opened, Jake forgot any manners she'd tried to instill in him, yanking against the leash as if to remind her there was a whole beach to explore with seagulls to harass and crabs to tease. She laughed and hurried to keep up with his pulling. The young dog was such a good companion for her at the lighthouse. Some days she still couldn't quite believe that she owned the small cottage with its attached landmark.

She paused to examine the crisp white trim and red roof. The small cottage suited her needs well. Sometime next year she hoped to turn the main floor of the lighthouse into a museum, but she still had work to do to get that scheme up and running. Something to occupy her during the long winter. With the daylight hours shortening, she'd have time in the evenings to work on the project.

Twenty minutes later her cheeks were flushed, her fingers frozen, and Jake disappointed when they returned to the cottage. She ate a quick breakfast then had her devotions before getting ready for the day. As she prayed, she couldn't ignore the tug to get back to the museum. She was missing something important. And the only way to learn what she'd overlooked was to return to the museum and see what she could find in the light of day. She prayed it was as simple as discovering the medal in a fold of the fabric they'd missed in the evening shadows. It was a practically impossible hope, but it didn't stop her from praying that locating the medal would be exactly that straightforward.

After making sure Jake had food and water, she headed to her car and drove to the museum, enjoying the way Vineyard Haven wasn't thronged with tourists as it had been when she'd first arrived. It was nice to find parking almost anytime now that the cooler weather had settled in. The road wound along like a tight, curvy maze. The last of the trees' vibrant leaves overhung the streets, protecting the small gingerbread houses along the way.

When she reached the East Shore Historical Museum, two vehicles waited in the parking lot, one of them Mildred's. Priscilla had wanted to arrive before anyone else, hoping to conduct another search with just Mildred in the building. Now that would have to wait for another day. She gathered her bag and locked the car before heading up the wide steps.

The bell tinkled above the door Priscilla entered, and a young woman turned and smiled at her. She had shoulder-length dark hair that was held back from her face by a lace headband and wore jeans with intentional holes and an oversized sweater. The cat eyeglasses made her look like she was trying hard to be taken seriously and reinforced the impression she might be a college student. She tilted her head and raised her eyebrow at Priscilla. "What are you doing here? We don't open for another hour."

Priscilla's shoulders straightened at the young woman's snide comment. "I came to talk to the director." Priscilla studied her, noting the pen stains around her fingertips on her right hand. "Who are you?"

"I'm Carly Kendricks, down from Boston for a week or so." She pointed toward the kitchen. "Ms. Pearson is in the kitchen. Muttered something about needing an IV of coffee this morning." Carly stepped closer and lowered her voice. "Have you heard about the excitement last night?"

"What excitement do you mean?"

"The big party. I've never been to a birthday party for someone turning one hundred. Were there a lot of people here?"

"I'd guess around eighty or so." Though the police should know for sure, considering the pages of their notebooks were filled with their cursory interviews.

Carly looked around the small museum as she clutched a folder to her chest. "That's a lot of people for such a small space. Was it fun?"

"It was until something went missing." She wanted to be vague about what was stolen, unsure what Mildred may have told this person.

"I heard someone stole a medal from one of the display cases."

So much for being evasive. "Last night was a bit rough."

"More than rough." The young woman pushed her glasses up on her nose, and the thick lenses made her eyes appear larger.

"True." Priscilla glanced at the display case, now pressed against a wall alongside the ticket counter. "I stood near the display case much of the evening. Many more people turned out than we'd expected."

"Once word got out about the birthday party, I'm sure everyone in town wanted to attend. Who wouldn't?" The young woman made no move. It was as if she were perfectly content just standing and talking to Priscilla.

"It was about as full as a tin of sardines." Priscilla crossed her arms and rubbed her sleeves, trying to warm up. "It's hard to imagine someone would have stolen the medal, but that's exactly what happened. I can't imagine why, though. It would only have value for Mrs. Spangler."

Carly frowned at her. "I doubt that. Many collectors love all things World War II. And to get their hands on a Congressional Gold Medal would be a coup."

"I guess I need to research the medal more."

"It would be a good idea. Might help you understand who would want it."

"Mildred and I cleaned up after the police and guests left, but we couldn't find it."

"So she said." Carly leaned closer. "I've been trying to tell her that the museum's security isn't good enough to protect all the important documents and photographs housed here. She isn't concerned."

Priscilla eyed the young woman. There was something familiar about her. Maybe without the thick glasses and her hair pulled back. Yes, she'd seen a young woman at the party who looked like her. But if she had been there, why ask so many questions? Why was she acting like she hadn't attended the event?

Priscilla stroked her chin. "So what brings you to the area?"

"I'm conducting research. Nothing interesting."

"Must be to entice you down here this time of year. I'm finding most avoid the island once the summer is over."

Carly smiled. "Oh, there are the fall tourists, but they're mostly leaving now too. It's the perfect time to visit, really—just as the fall tourists are leaving and before it gets too cold." She patted the expandable folder. "Well, it's time for me to get back to work. Nice to meet you."

"And you." Priscilla watched, a bit mystified as the girl strode away toward the stairs that led to the second-floor archives and research room. While she'd been friendly, she'd also been intentionally obtuse about what she was working on, and she'd seemed a little *too* friendly and a bit naive. Was it how she really saw the world, or had it been an act? If it was an act, why perform it with Priscilla? And was it possible Carly had attended the party last night?

Priscilla straightened a display of brochures as she watched the young woman leave, and Mildred walked into the room. "She's talkative," Priscilla commented to her friend.

"I'd call it something else—a nosy body." Mildred plopped on the wooden stool behind the small counter. "She talks my ear off about all the ways the museum isn't secure. It's like she thinks someone will wander in and steal something." Mildred's words seemed to register, and she covered her mouth with her hand. "I never imagined something like that would happen. What do we have here that anyone would find valuable enough to steal?"

"I'm sure you must have letters and documents of worth." *Maybe whoever stole the medal isn't planning on stopping there.* Priscilla didn't say the last part out loud.

"Maybe. But most people see them just as dusty old things." She rubbed the bridge of her nose. "I spend so much of my time convincing people that what we do matters, it's easy to forget that some people actually value what we have."

Priscilla pointed toward the stairs. "She seems interested."

"It's her job, but all the talk about security could drive me crazy. When she's in town, she's here almost every day we're open, and it's about the only conversation she knows."

Priscilla laughed at the exasperated expression on her friend's face. "It can't be that bad."

"You have no idea."

"She must be researching something interesting."

"I wouldn't know. She's treating her research like she's on some sort of secret treasure hunt. She's asked me to point her in the right direction but won't ask for input."

"It probably means she knows exactly what she needs."

Mildred snorted. "No one's that good. Conducting research in original, historic documents means a lot of digging, doubling back, trying again, and rabbit trails."

Priscilla thought about that as she heard the young woman's footsteps overhead in the research room. "Would she have taken the medal? It sounds like she wasn't here last night, but I thought I saw her."

"She says she wasn't here. I do remember that she left around noon yesterday. There were so many people last night that I wouldn't be able to tell you if she was here or not."

The front door dinged as a young couple walked inside. They looked to be in their late twenties, and their ruddy faces telegraphed they'd spent time at the shore even in the cooler temperatures.

Mildred pasted a smile on her face, but Priscilla noted the strain she couldn't quite hide. "Welcome to the East Shore Historical Museum."

"Thank you." The young man stepped forward and extended his hand to Mildred. "I'm Jack Rivers, and this is my wife, Melanie. We'd like to do some geology research while we're on the island, and Anna at the B&B suggested that we start here."

His wife stepped forward, her eyes shining. "We just got married and learned that one of Jack's ancestors may have been involved in the whaling industry on the island. We can't wait to see if it's true. It feels like a real-life mystery."

"Sounds like a fascinating honeymoon activity." Priscilla couldn't help responding to their excitement. If they were this passionate, then Mildred would need time to help them. She turned to her friend. "I'll come back later to chat." She smiled at the young couple, vividly remembering what it had been like when that was her and Gary. "Enjoy your time here. And enjoy each other. This is a magical time in your lives."

Melanie grinned. "That history degree might come in handy after all."

"Tell me more about your relative. I'll see how I can help you." Mildred led them to the parlor. "Have a seat while I get something to take notes on."

While she still had many questions about what had happened the prior night, Priscilla left knowing Mildred needed this time helping a couple explore their history. After some time with them, she'd be better prepared to tackle the disappearance of the medal and remember why she loved her job directing the museum. Perhaps Priscilla could start her own investigation by doing research on the Women Airforce Service Pilots and why someone would be so interested in that medal.

CHAPTER FIVE

The aroma of well-baked cookies stung Priscilla's nostrils, and she hurried into the kitchen, aware now that the oven timer had been beeping for a few minutes. She'd slipped so deeply into her morning Internet research, she'd completely tuned out the buzzer.

Priscilla turned off the timer, pulled on her oven mitt, and opened the oven door. The cookies weren't charred yet, but they were overbaked. Priscilla had made this no-fail chocolate chip recipe dozens of times, but she'd now discovered a way to cause them to fail: user error. Or rather: *user distraction.*

She had planned to research yesterday after she left the museum, but on her way home she'd received a call from Joan asking her to check on Trudy. She'd driven to Trudy's house to find her cousin in bed with a nasty cold. After making some homemade soup and doing some light housework for her cousin, she'd arrived home to Jake, who'd wanted all of her attention.

Priscilla had gotten up early to bake cookies for Trudy and finally get to that research. The cookie part hadn't turned out so well, but she'd learned some interesting information.

Using a spatula to slide the cookies off the cookie sheet, she deemed them good enough to dip in her morning coffee but not good enough for an ailing cousin whom she planned on visiting later in the afternoon. For Plan B, she would swing by Candy Lane Confectionery to pick up some goodies before heading to visit Trudy, who would perk up at the sight of a pastry from her favorite bakery.

As soon as the cookies were cooling, Priscilla turned back to the task that had distracted her in the first place—research about Women Airforce Service Pilots during World War II.

Easing into the dining room chair, she again turned her attention to the computer. With a resolved sigh, Jake plopped down at her feet.

"I know, I know. You're still waiting for your morning walk. But just five more minutes, I promise."

Over the last hour, she'd read numerous online articles about the women who flew military aircraft during World War II. She'd been both amazed by the bravery of the women and saddened to know how little they'd been honored over the years. After serving their country, flying military planes and risking their lives, they received no service pay. Upon their discharge, these women even had to pay for their bus rides home. Priscilla shook her head at the thought.

A grateful nation forgot to be grateful for almost seventy years.

It wasn't until 2010 that two hundred of these women, mostly in their late eighties and early nineties, were invited to the Capitol in Washington, DC, to receive the Congressional Gold Medal, the highest civilian honor bestowed by Congress. The joy in both the giving and the receiving of the award was clear in the photographs Priscilla found online.

The medal meant a lot to women like Deanie, who had volunteered to fly without expectation of being thanked. *Who would do such a thing to a precious veteran? Out of everything in the museum, why steal that?*

Priscilla closed her eyes and tried to picture the older woman as a young, eager pilot. It wasn't too hard to do. Even though Deanie no longer had a spring in her step, she had a twinkle in her eye. Priscilla couldn't imagine how heartbreaking it would be to have your medal stolen after waiting sixty-five years to receive it.

After reading a few more articles about the service pilots, she closed her laptop and rose. Jake jumped to his feet, his tail wagging furiously. Priscilla chuckled. "Okay, I'll take you on a walk." She moved to retrieve his leash. "But I hope you don't mind if I call Mildred on the way."

Priscilla walked outside with Jake and locked the cottage behind her. In the distance, ships chugged out to sea, preparing for their day's work. Tall masts of sailboats from a nearby harbor met the morning sun as it stretched its rays over the ocean. Taking in the view, she dialed Mildred's number and waited as it rang.

"Hello, this is Mildred."

"Mildred, this is Priscilla. I can't get that medal out of my thoughts. Do you know if there is anything else that's missing from the museum?" Carly's questions from the prior day wouldn't leave her alone.

"Anything else?" Mildred's voice rose an octave, revealing her panic. "I did try to look around, but there are so many places to look. I couldn't sleep last night. I keep replaying that hour between the time we last saw the medal and when we realized it was missing."

"If you need help going through things..."

"There was a corn-husk doll that I thought was missing, but I found it in a different place. I'll look around some more. I've decided to close for the day until I have a chance to look deeper. I even told Carly that she needed to take the day off." Her friend huffed out a breath. "Let me tell you, she wasn't too happy about that."

As she listened, Priscilla turned up the collar of her coat. The weather had turned cold, and a misty rain carried the aroma of seawater. One last rose quivered on the rosebush by the cottage, and Priscilla tried to imagine its new blooms in spring. At this moment spring seemed so very far away.

Jake tugged on the leash, leaping after a dry leaf. Priscilla tightened her grip and watched her step, making sure not to twist her ankle on the rocky ground. She was thankful for a break in the gray clouds overhead that let in a little sun. Still, the wind was biting cold and nipped at her nose.

"Could I help?" Priscilla offered. "I promise I won't touch anything unless you ask me to. How about I come by so you don't have to search alone?"

"Really? You'd do that?" Mildred's voice was as quiet as a whisper. No matter how tough the museum curator seemed on the outside, she was all marshmallow inside.

"Of course. And I'll bring lunch too—something simple. Will sandwiches and chips be all right?"

Mildred's sigh of relief echoed through the phone. "That sounds wonderful. I appreciate it."

Priscilla cut the walk short as the morning's to-do list ran through her mind. She'd make two quick lunches and then swing by Candy Lane's to get two boxes of pastries. Next, she'd go to the museum to help Mildred and then run the extra box of treats by Trudy's on the way home.

Back at her cottage, Priscilla stroked Jake's head and rubbed behind his ear with promises that they'd go on a longer walk the next day. After washing up, she pulled out the items she needed to make lunch. She made ham sandwiches with extra ham and crisp iceberg lettuce leaves—with just a touch of mayo—just like Gary liked them. Automatically, she grabbed two single-serving bags of sour cream and onion chips. When she and Gary first were married she hadn't liked that flavor of chips, but they'd grown on her over the years. And now that she no longer needed to buy them, it caused her heart to ache to think of not doing it.

As Priscilla put the chips into the paper bag, she felt tears in her eyes. It still surprised her sometimes how grief snuck up on her, causing her to get emotional over silly things like potato chips. But instead of moping, it helped to have friends she could help. After caring for Gary and her daughter all those years, it felt good to still be useful, even if she was in a new community.

Gathering all her things, she locked up the cottage and from the driver's seat paused to take in the view of the lighthouse before driving away. She didn't take the view for granted. It was breath-taking and so different from the panorama she'd grown used to in Kansas. While there was beauty to the rolling acres of farmland, there was a special beauty to the coastal view before her. The Lord had given her a fresh start and lots of interesting mysteries. These distracted her from dwelling on thoughts of the life she would have had if Gary were still with her.

Less than thirty minutes later, Priscilla had left one box of cream puffs in her car and carried another as she strode down the walkway to the museum. From down the road, the clock in the town square chimed, announcing noon.

Her cell phone rang, and Priscilla tugged it from her purse and noted Rachel's name on caller ID. "Hey, honey, can I call you back later? I just arrived at the museum—"

"Mom, I can't believe you didn't call me. I heard about the theft on the news."

"On the news? Do you mean the national news?"

"Yes, it's not every day a World War II pilot has a Congressional medal stolen. Were you there when it happened?"

Priscilla paused and lowered her head, the burden for the missing medal once again piling on her shoulders. "I was there. In fact..." She lowered her voice. "I was supposed to be watching the display. I feel responsible, which is why I'm going to help find the medal. If I hadn't been so distracted..."

"Mom..." Rachel's voice cut through the gloominess descending upon Priscilla. "It's not your fault. If a thief is determined to go after something, they'll do what they can to get it. You would never let this happen on purpose."

"Thank you, Rachel. That makes me feel better. I guess what I really feel is *concerned*." She paused. "You should have seen Mrs. Spangler's face when she realized the medal was gone. It broke my heart. I'm going to do my part to help."

Rachel chuckled. "Of course you are, Mom, but try to stay safe, all right? I'm hoping this is a one-time thing. To have that happen, in the midst of so many people, makes it seem like it was simply a crime of opportunity. And, yes, go ahead and say it. I've been watching too many crime shows."

Priscilla smiled, but her face was tight as she attempted to hold her emotions inside. Rachel's comment brought to mind so many nights when Gary had sat in his recliner watching any number of those shows. "Like father, like daughter."

"I'll take that." Rachel sighed. "And speaking of family, how are Joan, Gail, and Trudy handling all the excitement?"

"Well, Joan and Gail left yesterday to do some holiday shopping inland, and Trudy is under the weather. I made her some soup last night and will stop by later to see her with a box from Candy's."

"You better be careful. She might pretend to be sick more often."

Priscilla waved at Mildred who'd carried a broom out to the front porch to sweep. "Listen, I need to get going, but if I find anything, I'll let you know." How had word of the missing medal traveled all the way to her daughter? It must be a very slow news day.

As Priscilla entered the building, Mildred waited by the open door, relief on her face. Priscilla adjusted the sack lunches in her hand and gave Mildred a quick hug.

"Quite a crazy few days, huh?"

"You can say that again."

Mildred deposited the broom inside the janitor's closet, closed and locked the front door, and they walked to the kitchen. Both women picked at their sandwiches, and Mildred ignored the chips. She didn't seem interested in eating, and Priscilla didn't want to press her when there were so many questions hanging in the room.

After a few more minutes, Mildred pushed the food aside. "Thanks for bringing this, but I really can't eat. Guess I'm still too upset."

"Then let's get to work. The sandwiches will be fine if we decide we're hungry later."

It only took a minute to clean up, and then they got busy going through the items that would be of the most interest to a thief: arrowheads, a silver tea set, and Native American moccasins and a vest. Priscilla tried to make small talk as they worked, but it was clear Mildred's mind was preoccupied. Priscilla didn't want to press, but she had a few reservations about Carly that Mildred could clear up.

"How long have you known Carly?"

"Carly?" Mildred paused and ran her finger under her collar. Today she was wearing a wrap dress reminiscent of World War II.

"Since last year. She had a school project to do and needed information. She's a graduate student, I believe. Or maybe this is her senior year of college?" Mildred paused and stroked her chin. "I'm having a hard time remembering. She asks questions about so many things but rarely talks about herself."

Priscilla reached down to pick up a few crumpled napkins from the floor. "So did someone refer her to you?"

"Yes, a professor. She's a research assistant from Boston." Mildred scratched her head. "I can't remember if she was the one who was doing research for her professor's book or if that was another young woman." She sighed. "They all seem to talk more than anything else, always asking lots of questions."

"Carly was still here when I left yesterday. Did she stay long?"

"Oh yes, she stayed until I was ready to go. She said she didn't want me to be alone, which I thought was sweet."

Priscilla didn't answer. It was either sweet or sneaky. She didn't know enough about Carly to know which it was. Moving to the trash can, Priscilla threw away the napkins, noticing a clean liner. She glanced over her shoulder. "Did someone empty the trash from the party? From the Dumpster out back?"

Mildred paused and fiddled with her fake pearls. "You're the second one who's asked me that. Carly asked too. It was taken out—by the police actually. They came back after we had cleaned up and took the trash from the Dumpster for evidence. It's an old trick, I hear, to 'throw away' something valuable and then come back for it later."

Priscilla tapped her lip. "I've seen that on television." Emotion built in her throat as she thought of Gary and Rachel cuddled on the couch watching crime shows. It was one of their favorite things to do during their daughter's teen years. Priscilla quickly swallowed. "Cop shows used to be Gary's favorite."

Priscilla continued cleaning, lost in her thoughts. Oh, how Gary would have loved to be part of this. She could have asked his opinions of Carly, and he'd have a few. He'd always had a knack for seeing the person behind the mask.

She'd just turned to ask Mildred about what else the police had taken for evidence when a gasp carried from across the room. Mildred stood before a tall file cabinet. The middle drawer was open, and the older woman gazed down at the near-empty drawer with shock drawn across her face. "Nearly all the files from this drawer are missing!"

Priscilla hurried to Mildred's side. "What files are supposed to be in here?"

Mildred's voice shook. "Old ledgers from shipping routes. Nothing important. Nothing anyone would want to steal." She looked around the room at all the surfaces as if she'd just see the files lying there.

"Were they something Carly would be interested in?"

"I doubt it. There are much more valuable documents in this building. Old letters from important people. But shipping ledgers…I can't think of anyone who would want to take those. I'm positive they're just misplaced." She sounded like she was trying to convince herself. "They have to be here somewhere."

Mildred closed the drawer and sighed. "Should I report this to the police? They said to inform them of anything that I noticed out of place. Even though it's not peak season, we still stay busy. Visitors who come to see the fall colors often stay to conduct family research while they're here. For all I know one of their ancestors could have been the captain of a ship included in those ledgers. Yes, I'm sure those files were just put in the wrong spot."

Priscilla listened, but she wasn't sure. She ran her hand through her shoulder-length hair. "You should call the police, and we'll keep looking. I have another hour I can help before I check on Trudy." Which also meant that Priscilla had another hour to wonder about those files.

As she worked, she couldn't shake the thought of how odd it was that these particular files were the ones missing. *Why would anyone be interested in old ships' logs and information about shipping lanes?*

CHAPTER SIX

Later that afternoon, rays of sunlight dared to puncture the dark clouds, sending beams of light down to Misty Harbor. Priscilla fixed her eyes out the window and noticed a sightseeing plane doing a low, lazy circle in the sky. She imagined the pilot providing the history of the Misty Harbor Lighthouse to his passengers. What stories did he tell? Did he share about the newest occupant who was more oriented to waves of golden grain than waves of glimmering water? Did he talk about the WASP pilot and the missing medal?

As Priscilla watched the plane, she imagined a similar plane decades ago with a youthful, eager young woman in the cockpit. She imagined Deanie letting out a whoop during her first solo flight. As a young girl, had Deanie even considered such a thing possible?

Life has a way of taking all types of twists and turns. The thought resonated in her heart. Her life had certainly taken turns she hadn't foreseen, and she was glad she hadn't. If she'd known what was coming, she wasn't sure she would have followed the course life had mapped out for her.

Jake nudged her thigh with his nose. She looked down at him. "It seems you're ready for a walk, as always." She chuckled. "I can't imagine how sedentary I'd be if you didn't push me all the time."

Jake's energetic tail thumped, and she patted his head. "Good boy for making me interact with life and not get stuck in my head too much."

She pulled on a jacket and zipped it to her neck, then she put Jake on his leash. The air was warmer than she expected, and the warm breeze tossed leaves around the yard.

"Keep blowing, toss those leaves into the sea." Priscilla chuckled. Then shook her head. *Don't I wish?* She knew what she'd spend tomorrow doing, making this place sparkle for the weekend's tour. Once a week, on Saturdays, Teresa Claybrook's tour company came by and gave tours of the lighthouse. Every tour so far, the eighteen-seat minibus had been full. For now, the cottage and gardens were off-limits, but Priscilla liked the idea of the tours expanding.

"Don't rush things, Mom," Rachel had urged her. Sometimes it felt as if the roles had been reversed, with Rachel becoming the mother and she the child. Yet Priscilla felt it was right to share all she'd been given, including the lighthouse.

For now, she'd gotten used to the bus arriving every week. Sometimes she watched as the tourists climbed from the bus, taking joy in their excitement. She was under no obligation to keep her cottage in pristine shape, but she liked to make the experience as wonderful for the visitors as possible. There had been a few times when people had peeked in through a window, and it was nice to know they'd see a clean space. If nothing else, it gave her a weekly deadline for having the place spick-and-span.

She remembered the last time she'd visited was during the late fall. It was like a new discovery. Most of the tourists had left, and there was a grayness that settled over the place—not only outside but within her aunt's home. What was supposed to be a happy Thanksgiving turned into anything but.

When Priscilla was young, she hadn't understood the disagreement between her mother and aunt. Sometimes it was still hard knowing what happened. But coming back to Martha's Vineyard had forged a way of reconnecting, of reconciling. Priscilla knew she was here for a reason, even though the exact reason remained elusive. Maybe it was more than one reason. Maybe God would show her over time.

Jake tugged on the leash, pulling Priscilla from her thoughts. She noticed a woman in the distance. The woman was walking toward them on the trail from the beach to the cottage. She lifted her hand and waved, as if it were a meet up between old friends. Priscilla tilted her head, wondering if she had met this woman before. Had the woman attended the birthday party for Deanie? She didn't think she recognized her, but it could be possible. It was hard to see the woman under her wide sun hat.

The woman smiled as she approached. She wore a jean jacket flecked with paint and a gray-blue scarf that matched her smiling eyes.

"Good afternoon, Priscilla."

At Priscilla's side, Jake wagged his tail and tugged to reach the woman, as if he'd just discovered a long-lost friend.

"I'm sorry. Do I know you?"

"Most likely not. We haven't met before." Laughter spilled from the woman's lips. "But everyone in town knows you—or knows *of you* at least. Many people have had their eye on this lighthouse. It's such a beautiful spot, don't you think?"

"Yes, it is." Priscilla's shoulders relaxed. "I suppose the story of a woman from Kansas inheriting this much-loved lighthouse gets spread around town, doesn't it?"

"That and the fact that you've already been so helpful to others here." The woman shrugged. "If I'd just moved from a different place, I would have been tempted to hide. I'm glad you haven't done that."

A cold wind picked up. It pressed against the woman's back, causing her short grayish-blonde curls to whip into her face. Her smile was warm, and her eyes were bright with life. She stepped forward and stroked Jake's head, and Priscilla liked her immediately. Rachel's warning about not allowing strangers into her cottage flew through her thoughts, but she quickly pushed it away.

Priscilla rubbed her arms, trying to warm up. "Won't you come in? The wind is picking up. It does this every day, attempting to blow ancient sailing ships to shore."

"Yes, I'd love to come in. Thank you for the invitation." The woman matched her stride to Priscilla's as they walked to the cottage. With his tail still wagging, Jake led the way. "I'm Lillian Salisbury."

"Nice to meet you, Lillian." Priscilla paused and extended her hand. "As you know, I'm Priscilla, and this handsome boy is Jake."

The sound of waves mixed with their footsteps. As she walked, Priscilla studied the seaside cottage with its weathered, sea-blue clapboard siding and white trim, the windows flanked by bright white shutters and garnished with flower boxes, now empty. The lighthouse loomed over the cottage, punching into the gray fog that rolled in. *Home, sweet home.* She was still getting used to the idea, and it seemed as if those around town were too.

Once inside, Lillian took off her jacket and hung it over the back of a kitchen chair. Then she ran her fingers through her curls, as if attempting to control them, but if anything, her actions caused them to puff up more fully.

Lillian barely glanced around the cottage. Instead she moved to the front window, taking in the view of the land, the sand, and the gray sea. "Do you like living here? Do you miss the mainland too much?"

Priscilla moved to heat water for tea. "I do love it. Although there were times I wondered if I would, being a Kansas prairie girl and all." She reached into the cupboard and pulled out a package of cookies. It was something her mother had taught her—to always keep cookies on hand for unexpected company. After her cookie-baking debacle, it might be a while before she tried fresh cookies again. "I've found that I have everything I really need right here. I've never been one for malls or big box stores. I forget at times I'm not connected to the mainland. It's such a beautiful place."

"It is a beautiful place, which is why I've come. Could I paint the lighthouse?"

Priscilla paused putting cookies on a plate. "Paint it? I'm not sure. You'd have to ask the Coast Guard. They're the ones who have a contract to—"

Laughter spilled from the woman's lips, and she pulled herself away from the view and turned back to Priscilla. "No, not paint it that way. I'm a watercolor artist. I paint on canvas—mostly landscapes—I've never quite mastered painting people well."

Priscilla's laughter joined Lillian's. "Of course, that makes so much more sense." She set the plate of cookies on the table and placed an open palm to her forehead. "I'm not sure what I was thinking."

Lillian reached for her jacket where it hung on the chair and pulled a package of note cards from an inner pocket. She handed the package to Priscilla, who opened it and looked through them. Each card depicted various scenes from around the island. Trinity Park Tabernacle, Old Whaling Church, and Aquinnah Cliffs. Priscilla recognized the popular landmarks from her drives around the island.

"You painted these?"

"Yes, those note cards were made from prints of my paintings. It's my goal to paint more scenes from around the island. My husband and I used to live part of the year in New Bedford, on the mainland, but now he's retired and we've decided to stay here year-round. A few years ago I started painting Martha's Vineyard's landmarks, but mostly in the summer. Being here in the fall—with winter coming— it's as if I've discovered a whole new world. Your lighthouse was at the top of my new list of places to paint."

"I don't mind at all. Did you plan to set up in front of the cottage?"

"Yes, but not too close. I might set up at the very edge of your property where the land meets the sand."

Priscilla set the steeping tea on the table. "In that case, why did you even feel the need to ask? Not that I mind getting to know you, but while I own the buildings, I don't own the view."

Lillian sat and poured herself a cup of tea, adding a spoonful of honey and stirring slowly. "I didn't want to worry you, some strange woman with an easel out there for a few days, as if I'm watching you." She chuckled and then took a careful sip of her tea, the steam rising around her face.

"I would have figured it out, but feel free to use my property. And if you need to warm up or use the restroom, feel free to come to the door. I'm usually home, unless some bit of excitement around town is pulling me away."

"There has been some excitement in town, hasn't there? Have you heard about that stolen Congressional Gold Medal? That's so awful. You weren't there, were you?" She took another sip. "I don't understand how something that precious could be stolen in the midst of all those people. Didn't they have someone watching it?" The woman cocked an eyebrow and narrowed her gaze. "I mean, with something so important you'd think they would have paid more attention to security." Then Lillian leaned close. "You don't know more about the stolen medal, do you?"

The woman's eyes pierced Priscilla's, and suddenly Priscilla wondered if she'd done the right thing. Was it safe letting a stranger come into her house like this? And did the woman really want to paint her lighthouse, or had she come to learn more about the medal?

The woman looked harmless enough. But how could Priscilla know if Lillian was the painter of these note cards? Was a paint-splattered jacket enough evidence? And did watercolors even splatter like that?

Priscilla wanted to give Lillian the benefit of the doubt. "There's not much more I know about the medal, but tell me . . . what time of day do you plan on coming? I imagine the light shines differently throughout the day."

"Sometime in the morning. I love the way the lighthouse sits on its perch. With the cloud cover like it is, the light shouldn't change much."

Priscilla placed a cookie on the napkin in front of her. "Well, I can't wait to see the finished painting."

Lillian smiled. "You won't have to wait long. Just as long as it's not raining, I should finish within the week."

"Well, I should be here . . ." Priscilla let her voice trail off. She was about to say, *unless I can figure out a way to help find the missing medal*, but she decided to leave the last part out. She'd only just met Lillian and felt she needed to protect what she knew about the search for the medal. It seemed to her the fewer people who knew about their search, the more likely they'd find it. Or at least that was her hope.

Lillian stayed for a second cup of tea, and they talked mostly about island living and the peace each felt as they listened to the waves crashing against the shore.

"I read a scripture verse just the other day," Priscilla commented, "about how the Lord gave the seas a boundary that cannot be crossed. It's good to know that if the Lord can hold back that powerful water out there, He can keep back the waves that threaten to crash into our lives."

Lillian nodded, taking in Priscilla's words. "I haven't read the Bible much, but I like that. It's something I'd like to share with my husband."

"Here, let me write it down for you." Priscilla rose and moved to retrieve her Bible, a pen, and a notebook. "It was in Jeremiah chapter five, I believe."

She found the verse and wrote it down, handing it to Lillian.

"'Should you not fear me?' declares the Lord. 'Should you not tremble in my presence?'" Lillian read. "'I made the sand a boundary for the sea, an everlasting barrier it cannot cross. The waves may roll, but they cannot prevail; they may roar, but they cannot cross it.'" Her eyes narrowed as she read those words, and a crease formed in her brow. "I, uh, don't know what to say. Thank you."

Tension tightened in Priscilla's gut. "It's something special that I read..."

"I, uh, I have a feeling that I need to read more like this." Lillian patted the note cards that were sitting on the table. "And I'd love to leave these with you."

"Thank you, but are you sure? I can't wait to send notes to friends back home. I've been urging so many of them to come for a visit. Maybe this will do the trick."

"Yes, I'm sure." Lillian looked around, as if seeing the interior of the cottage for the first time. Then she took in a deep breath. "I needed today—needed this time." She patted the paper with the verse on it. "Thank you, Priscilla, thank you." She rose. "I'm look-ing forward to seeing you tomorrow."

Priscilla followed Lillian to the door, watching as she buttoned up her jacket. With more promises to connect tomorrow, Lillian rushed back to the path, as if trying to outrun the wind. And just as she watched the woman walking away, Priscilla's phone rang. She checked the caller ID. Her heartbeat quickened to see that it was Mildred.

"Mildred? Is everything all right?"

"I didn't know who to call. This is my weekend to sit with my mother. My sister needs the break, but I can't stop thinking about everything we looked through. Do you remember if the old copies of the *London Chronicle* were in the filing cabinet in the kitchen? There's one from 1777. That might be of value to someone."

"I don't remember, but if you like, I can come by the museum tomorrow and help you check."

"I would appreciate the help. You're the only one I know for certain didn't take the medal. You're the only one I can trust."

Unfortunately, except for her cousins, Mildred, and the authori-ties, Priscilla felt exactly the same way.

"When you arrive at the museum, I think I know where we should look for the paper," Mildred continued. "It's about a naval skirmish here on Martha's Vineyard during the Revolutionary War."

"Sounds fascinating." Priscilla considered the best way to calm her friend's nerves. "Don't worry about it now. So far, except for those shipping logs, we haven't found anything missing. I'm sure we'll learn those were simply misplaced."

From the other end of the line, Mildred released a long exhale. "Thank you, Priscilla. I really appreciate it. After talking to you, I'll be able to sleep tonight."

"Sleep is important. Sweet dreams, friend." As she hung up, Priscilla wished the same for herself. As the anniversary of Gary's death neared, she had a harder time getting to sleep at night. As she lay in the dark, her mind took her back to the last days when her strong husband wilted before her eyes and he could barely lift his head. She placed her phone on the counter and plugged in the charger as tears filled her eyes. When she'd said, *"Until death do us part,"* so many years ago, she hadn't thought it would end like that. She'd been so eager for the life she would build with Gary, she hadn't considered life without him.

A few hours later as she got ready for bed, her mind drifted to Gerald, the handsome Coast Guard captain she was getting to know. She pushed thoughts of him away. As much as she liked the idea of spending time with such a nice man, she couldn't imagine opening her heart again. Yes, she was open to friendships. She was looking forward to helping Mildred and even getting to know Lillian over the coming days. But she had loved one man with all her heart, and she couldn't imagine doing that again. She was thankful for one man to spend her life with...and she'd trust God to bring in good relationships to give her companionship over the coming years.

CHAPTER SEVEN

The museum was quiet as Priscilla stood in the archives room and searched through file cabinets. There were so many newspaper articles protected in clear sleeves, how would she find the one that Mildred was concerned about? Her friend had led her to a section and then headed back downstairs to help a small group of tourists. Priscilla had found stories from the *Boston Globe*, the *New England Chronicle*, and even the *New York Times*. Someone had been faithful over the years to search several newspapers for stories about Martha's Vineyard and then take the time to clip them out and preserve them.

As she continued to thumb through the articles, she finally found the story Mildred was talking about from the *London Chronicle* dated January 8, 1777. It was hard to read, mostly because the *s*'s looked like *f*'s. "We failed from New York on the 17th of November on a cruife. We put into Martha'f Vineyard, and fent our boat on fhore with a flag of truce." Priscilla chuckled at the odd phrasing then set it aside to show to Mildred when she returned. She had to agree with Carly. If there were items that Mildred was worried about losing, shouldn't more be done concerning security around this place?

She flipped through a few more articles. They seemed to be filed by type of event rather than date. Stories from the Revolutionary War were filed with stories from World War II. Thinking of Deanie, she paused on a story from the *Vineyard Gazette* from December 26, 1941.

> One of the victims of the Japanese surprise attack upon the Philippines on Dec. 7 was John H. Campbell, son of Mr. and Mrs. Fred P. Campbell of New Britain and Oak Bluffs. He had spent all of his summers at Oak Bluffs, except that of 1941, and he had many friends in the town and among the summer colony. He enlisted in the US Army Air Corps in 1940, and would have soon qualified as a pilot after training in the fundamentals of aviation. Mr. Campbell was born in New Britain and was educated in the public schools there, being graduated from the high school in 1938.

Priscilla slid the protected sheet back into the file cabinet and recalled some of the stories she'd overheard Deanie talking about with her birthday guests. She too spent her summers in Oak Bluffs. Since John and Deanie were around the same age, Priscilla had no doubt they knew each other. The population wasn't that big back then. She'd also learned from Deanie's stories that Clark Field in the Philippines had been bombed just eight hours after Pearl Harbor. That's something most people didn't learn in the history books. Yet Deanie knew it because she'd lived it.

I've been going about this all wrong. Priscilla closed the file cabinet drawer. "I've been poking around trying to find information about the medal," she whispered to herself, "but what I need to do is go to the source."

She paused and tried to remember where Andrew had said his aunt lived. It was someplace in town. An assisted-living facility? *Vineyard Village.* The name popped in her head, and she remembered seeing its sign not far from the Long Point Wildlife Refuge beach. On a whim she called to see if she could visit Deanie. The receptionist said Deanie would have lunch in fifteen minutes in the cafeteria, and she always enjoyed guests. That was all the invitation Priscilla needed. Within a few minutes she was parking her car and hurrying up to the home's visitor entrance while also trying to outrun the wind. When she entered, the receptionist asked Priscilla to sign in and place a visitor's sticker on her sweater.

Priscilla followed the receptionist down a long hall with white-and-green tile squares and an aroma of home cooking. *Meatloaf, definitely meatloaf,* she thought with a smile.

They entered the cafeteria, and Priscilla spotted Deanie right away. Her wheelchair was pushed to the side. She was sitting in a regular dining room chair and talking with a gentleman. There was an empty spot next to her on the other side, and Priscilla decided to take her chances and ask if she could join them.

With a wave forward from the receptionist, Priscilla approached. "Excuse me, Deanie. Is it all right if I join you?"

Deanie looked up, and at first there was a blank expression on her face.

"I'm sorry to interrupt, but I was just checking to see how you were doing after your birthday party. I know there was a lot of excitement. It was quite the shock."

Recognition dawned on Deanie's face. "You were the lady who was there. The one who was watching over everything."

Priscilla's smile fell. "I suppose I was. Or at least trying. I didn't do a very good job, did I?"

Deanie didn't respond. Instead she just patted the chair beside her. "Sit, please."

Priscilla did as she was told, suddenly worried that she made a mistake coming here. Did Deanie blame her? The sad look in the elderly woman's eyes was hard to miss.

Deanie leaned forward and narrowed her gaze. "Now listen here. I want you to know that what happened is *not* your fault. There was so much excitement, so many things happening…It would have been impossible for someone to concentrate on watching the medal. Besides, in a place like Vineyard Haven, things are usually safe." Deanie reached over and placed a hand on top of Priscilla's. "It's just a thing. I'm sorry that it will not be at the historical museum, but it's still only a thing."

Priscilla's jaw dropped. A mix of thankfulness and sadness filled her chest. The same emotions she felt many years ago when she had accidentally thrown a baseball through a neighbor's window surged through her. She'd been thankful the neighbor was understanding, but still sad at her mistake. Just like then, she wished she could go back and do things differently. Unfortunately, life didn't work like that.

"How can you say it's just a *thing*… " Emotion caught in Priscilla's throat. She heard a gentle snore and looked over to see Deanie's lunch partner snoozing in his wheelchair, his chin to his chest.

Seeing him lightened the moment. The emotion released, and laughter slipped from Priscilla's lips.

Deanie reached over and patted the older gentleman's hand. "Howard here used to be part of the 11th Armored Division. Some days when he's doing well, he can tell you about his involvement in the Battle of the Bulge and liberating a concentration camp. You can't live through those times and cling too strongly to things."

"But it was so important. The medal was given to you at the Capitol."

Deanie tapped her temple. "And I still have the memory...today at least." She chuckled.

Priscilla looked around. At each table people sat and talked. There were no smartphones or tablets open in front of them. They had no place to go and not much to do, but they had each other, and they seemed perfectly content with that.

Deanie picked up her biscuit, buttered it, and took a bite. Priscilla could tell by the look in her eyes that she had something important to say. "As the end of my life nears, the things that I've accumulated don't have much meaning. When I moved out of my house, I gave so much away." She sighed. "Less to dust. Less to clean. What I enjoy most now are days like today when I can spend time with friends, which means you too, young lady."

"I like the thought that you consider me a friend." Priscilla smiled. "And I like being called 'young lady' too."

"I always have room for one more friend. At my age I've lost so many on earth. I can tell you there will be so many reunions when

I reach heaven. Between friends I lost last month and friends I lost seventy years ago, it'll be quite a party."

Priscilla scooted herself closer to Deanie. "Did you lose any female pilot friends during the war?"

"I'm sorry to say I did." She looked up at the ceiling and blinked slowly, as if seeing faces in her mind. "Thirty-eight WASPs lost their lives in the war. I knew three of them personally. Jane, Dolores, Claire. They were all sweet girls. Claire was a mother. She left a young son..."

An attendant came by and asked if he could take Deanie's tray. She'd hardly touched her food, but from the look on her face, her mind wasn't on her lunch. "All of us had the same training as the male cadets. I mostly ferried airplanes, flying them from one place to another. But some of my friends towed targets."

"Towed targets? Please tell me that doesn't mean what I think it means."

"Of course it does. Women pulled targets behind their planes for men to shoot artillery at. Most of them hit the targets, but sometimes they missed the target...that's how Claire lost her life."

Priscilla shook her head. "You know, I consider myself an educated woman, but how come I haven't heard these stories before?"

Deanie waved her hand, as if brushing off her concerns. "There is so much that happened in the war. There were so many heroes. But for us, we were just doing our part."

Priscilla considered her words. "I only hope that if we were to face the same thing today, we'd all rise to the occasion like you did."

"Don't underestimate people. That's what the medal meant to me—my chance to share our story in hopes that it would inspire someone else's. All I want is that my story won't die with me. I want others to remember the contributions of my friends—most of them gone. I want them to understand the courage it took for us women to step forward and do what most people believed was a man's job—and to remember after the last WASP is gone. I have to trust that God can make that happen without my medal. If anything, this is a faith moment."

There was a stirring within the cafeteria. Priscilla looked around and noted that attendants were removing trays and clearing the tables. Others were helping residents back to their rooms. Priscilla knew her time with Deanie was nearing an end, but she had a couple more questions to ask.

"Deanie, may I ask you what you meant by saying this is a faith moment?"

"Oh yes, it's a term I've used for many years after I heard it in a sermon." Deanie's voice had a little wobble to it now, and Priscilla knew she must be getting tired, but Priscilla could also see the flash of joy in the older woman's eyes as she explained. "You see, we humans often see life's challenges as a hard thing—something we wish wouldn't happen—but God goes out of His way to give us moments that exercise our faith."

"I'm sure you've had so many moments like that in your life."

Deanie folded her wrinkled hand on the table in front of her. "Yes, I have. And when I have to take a step of faith and trust God, He always shows up one way or another. After one hundred years on this earth, I can't say He shows up in ways that I expect or want, but He always reveals part of Himself. There were times in those airplanes when I found myself in quite a pickle. Once, I got caught in a tornado over Kansas. Another time I had an engine fail, and I had to crash land. After that, anytime I faced hardship during my life I'd think back to those moments. I knew that if God could protect me then, everything else I had to face was a breeze.

"When God exercises our faith, He does so to bless us. Or to bless the church and remind His people of His presence. Or maybe He does it even as a witness to unbelievers, which I'm hoping for here. I've been praying for my great-nephew for many years...maybe God will somehow use this." Deanie sighed. "I have faith that He will."

The contentment on the woman's face was hard to miss, and Priscilla hoped she could have the same type of trust in God's perfect plan someday. This woman couldn't get around like she used to. Her body was failing her. She'd been forced to walk away from her home, and now she was a victim of theft, yet her clear blue eyes, rimmed with fresh tears, weren't looking toward all that was wrong. Instead, she was staring ahead into the future, attempting to see how God was about to make everything right.

"Thank you for sharing that. I just have one more question. Before your birthday event, was there anyone recently who came asking about the medal? Maybe someone with whom you'd shared about your upcoming donation to the museum?"

Deanie furrowed her brow as if trying to think. "The police asked me that question the other night, and I couldn't think of anyone. Mildred and I agreed we wanted it to be a fun surprise.

But just this morning I did remember someone. Willow Gibson." She said the name as if Priscilla should know who it was.

"Willow Gibson?"

"Yes, she owns Silver Willow down in Vineyard Haven. She called me about a week or two ago and asked me all kinds of questions about my medal. She's such a nice lady. So smart. When we talked, it seemed she knew more about the medal than even I did."

Priscilla was about ask Deanie what she meant by that when the sound of footsteps approached from behind. Priscilla assumed it was an attendant coming to help Deanie back to her room. Instead a famliar voice interrupted their conversation.

"Aunt Deanie." Andrew Wright's voice was sharp. "Who are you talking to?"

Priscilla turned, and the smile fell from her face. Even though Andrew was again dressed like a model stepping out of a J.Crew catalog, his face wrinkled in displeasure.

"Oh, I'm Priscilla." She pushed back her chair and stood. "You may not remember, but we met the other night..."

"I remember. Perhaps I misspoke. Aunt Deanie, *why* are you talking to this woman? Didn't the police tell you they are working on finding your medal?"

Priscilla folded her arms over her chest. "I'm sorry. I didn't realize this was a problem." Andrew narrowed his gaze, and she pulled her arms tighter against her waist and shrugged. "I was just hoping to help."

He cleared his throat and shifted his weight from one foot to the other. "If you wanted to help, then maybe you should have done something sooner—something to ensure the medal wasn't stolen in the first place." He took another step closer. "Now, tell me why you're really here."

Priscilla turned to look at Deanie. The older woman's eyes were wide, and her voice shook. "Andrew, please calm down. This is my friend."

"Please, Aunt, just because you've known someone a few days doesn't make them a friend. What happened the other night should have proven that. We have no idea what Priscilla's true motives are."

Priscilla attempted to lean closer to Deanie to tell her that she should just go, but Andrew squared his shoulders, scooting closer and shoving himself between them. It was obvious that he didn't want anyone near his aunt. The question was, why? What was he trying to hide?

CHAPTER EIGHT

Priscilla arrived home and parked the car. Both thankfulness and worry filled her mind. Thankfulness for all Deanie had shared about faith moments and worry that there was a reason Andrew Wright didn't want his aunt speaking with anyone. Could Andrew be behind this? But why? What would be his motivation?

She turned off the ignition and paused for a moment, trying to remember how Andrew had acted at the birthday party. He'd been present but aloof. He'd hung around his aunt, as if monitoring her, but when they'd pulled back the velvet fabric and saw that the medal was missing, he hadn't been around. Where had he gone? Could he have taken the medal while no one was watching? Priscilla didn't know what his motive would be, but unlike the rest of the guests, he knew it was there. He knew its value too.

As Priscilla climbed from her car, she noticed another car parked near the path to the ocean. She didn't recognize it, but it wasn't uncommon for visitors to park there in order to walk along the shore.

Red and orange leaves skittered across the sidewalk to the cottage. She shut the car door and pulled her jacket tighter around her. She was halfway to the house when she noticed something far off where her meadow neared the cliff's edge. Priscilla paused and looked closer. It was an easel. A painter's easel. She looked at the parked car again, and then she remembered. It had to be Lillian's easel. Lillian's car. She said she'd be coming to paint.

Jake's barking came from the house, but something told Priscilla not to go in. Not yet. If Lillian's car was here and her easel was here, Lillian had to be also. But where?

Priscilla started walking down the path toward the easel. As she did she heard another vehicle. She turned to see a familiar SUV. It was a Coast Guard vehicle. It parked, and she recognized the driver. Gerald O'Bannon was wearing his uniform, but with the chill in the air he wore a navy-blue jacket. He waved as he climbed from his SUV and pointed at the lighthouse, holding up a clipboard. So this wasn't a social call. Priscilla waved back. The polite thing to do would be to go greet him. A slight smile tipped her lips. She liked the idea of that. She always enjoyed talking with Gerald. But even as much as she wanted to talk to him, something didn't feel right about the easel. Something told her to go check it out. So Priscilla gave one last wave to Gerald and then hurried across the field toward the easel.

Priscilla heard the woman's low moan before she saw her. Then she noticed the familiar jean jacket and a red scarf. "Lillian?" Priscilla rushed forward.

Lillian was lying on the ground. She attempted to sit up, but she couldn't quite make it. Her eyes were wide, and her lower lip quivered. She reached toward her leg, and Priscilla noted her foot was twisted at a strange angle.

Priscilla knelt beside her. "Are you all right?" She took Lillian's hand, so very cold, in her own.

Lillian sat with Priscilla's help and grasped Priscilla's arm. "I'm afraid I've hurt my ankle." Tears rimmed her eyes. "I was setting up my easel and paints and didn't see that hole until it was too late and I'd stepped in it." She touched her ankle and winced. "I'm not sure if I broke it. Or maybe I tore a ligament, but I tried to get up, and, well, that made it worse."

"I'll go get help. How long have you been here?"

"I'm not sure. Maybe an hour? Maybe more?"

"Oh, Lillian. Stay right here. I have a friend at the lighthouse right now. I'll run and get him. Unless you want me to call an ambulance."

"Not an ambulance. I just need some help up..."

"I don't think I could help you all by myself. But I know my friend can help."

Priscilla pulled off her jacket and wrapped it around Lillian's shoulders. Then she stood and hurried back the way she came. She half walked, half ran to the lighthouse. She was out of breath when she rushed up the steps and through the door.

Priscilla had only taken two steps inside when she ran into something. It was Gerald. The force of hitting against him caused her to stumble back. Two strong arms reached around her, steadying her. Priscilla found her footing and tried to breathe, tried to still her pounding heart.

"Whoa there. Steady yourself. Is everything all right?" The words tumbled out of Gerald's mouth. "You're shivering." He quickly took off his jacket and wrapped it around her shoulders, a gesture that mirrored what she'd done for Lillian. Had Lillian felt as protected as she did? "Is everything all right, Priscilla?"

"I'm fine." She stepped back and fingered his jacket. She was about to insist he take it back but realized she was cold and slid her arms into the sleeves instead.

"It's my friend Lillian. She came today to paint the lighthouse. She set up her easel by the cliff's edge and then tripped in a hole. I'm not sure if her ankle is broken, but she's been out there for an hour at least. Her ankle is twisted at an odd angle too. Can you help me get her to my car? I need to get her to urgent care."

"Yes, of course. Where is she?"

"You'll see the easel. She's right beside it."

"I'll go. You stay here and catch your breath." Priscilla nodded. She stepped to the side, and Gerald hurried out the door. She took a moment to catch her breath and then followed him. By the time she caught up, Gerald was kneeling at Lillian's side. He gently probed her ankle.

"I'm not an expert, but it looks broken to me." He turned to Priscilla as she approached. "Instead of going to urgent care, head straight to the hospital. They have an orthopedic doctor there."

Priscilla nodded. "Yes. I'll do that."

Lillian moaned. "I'm sorry to be such a bother. My husband told me it wasn't a good day for painting. And then I went and left my phone in the car with my purse. I couldn't even call him."

Priscilla patted her arm. "Don't worry. We're here now."

Gerald looked at Lillian. "The hard part will be getting you up. I think if I step around behind you and grab you from under your arms... Yes, that will work."

Priscilla stepped closer too. "I'll help steady her as she stands."

Gerald lifted Lillian from behind. The wind tossed Lillian's curls into his face, but he didn't seem bothered. Once Lillian was up, Priscilla stepped closer and slid her arm under Lillian's and around her back. Lillian put an arm around Priscilla, leaning on her for support while making sure she didn't put any weight on her left ankle. Gerald moved to the other side, and Lillian wrapped an arm around his shoulders too.

"I am so embarrassed..."

Priscilla righted herself, trying to keep her hold as Lillian attempted to hop forward. "Don't be. I'm glad we could help."

Lillian tried to hop forward again, but it was hard to keep her steady. She seemed weak, as if the ordeal and the cold had sapped all her energy.

"Wait up." Gerald paused, looking from Lillian to Priscilla and back to Lillian again. "We could call an ambulance, but it'll take fifteen minutes to get here. Ma'am, if you don't mind, can I carry you to the car?"

"I wouldn't ask that. I'm much too heavy."

He chuckled. "At work we have to do drills all the time. You're much lighter than the recruits I carry over my shoulders... not that I'm going to carry you that way."

"Well, I don't want to be a bo—"

Without waiting for her to finish, Gerald scooped Lillian up—like a groom would carry a bride over the threshold—and strode to the car. Priscilla's jaw dropped as she watched him go. The man never ceased to amaze her. He carried Lillian as if he were carrying a sack of potatoes.

Priscilla quickly gathered up the easel and Lillian's other things then followed them. By the time she got to the car, Lillian was already reclining across Priscilla's back seat.

Gerald pointed to the things in Priscilla's hands. "If you leave those, I'll put them in Lillian's car."

"Would someone mind getting my purse from my car?" Lillian's voice carried pain in it. "I'll need my insurance card and ID."

"I'll grab that for you, ma'am." In a minute Gerald was back with a purse that he passed through the window to Lillian.

"Thank you."

"No problem. Anything else you ladies need?" His gaze locked with Priscilla's.

"Would you mind letting Jake out for me? He's been in the house all day."

Gerald stepped back from the car. "I can do that. Is the spare key still where your aunt left it?"

Priscilla's brow furrowed. "Yes, it is." Had he known about the spare key this whole time? She supposed it made sense. Of course her aunt would have trusted Gerald. He might have helped her too. If he was around a lot, he no doubt did. Priscilla thanked him again and started the car.

Lillian spoke from the back seat. "Thank you so much for doing this. I feel so horrible, interrupting your day like this."

"Helping a friend is not an interruption. I feel bad you lay there so long without help." Priscilla turned up the heater, turning the vents so the warm air was directed to Lillian.

"I should've listened when Al told me to wait until a nicer day to paint."

"Have you called him yet?" Priscilla pulled onto the main road. "Wait, you couldn't because you didn't have your phone. Maybe you should call him now. Ask him to meet us at the hospital."

"I will as soon as my teeth stop clattering." Lillian chuckled. "I'm not sure I'll reach him since it's chore time. He'll be out in the barn with all the animals, and he's horrible about carrying his cell phone. He said he hasn't needed one for seventy years, why need it now?"

Sure enough, Lillian tried to call Al, but he didn't pick up. She left a message and tucked the phone back in her purse. "I'm not sure he knows how to check his voice mail."

It was only after Priscilla had driven a few miles that she realized she was still wearing Gerald's jacket. What would she have done if he hadn't been there? She didn't want to think about that.

Priscilla parked the car outside of the Emergency Room entrance. "Don't worry. We'll get a hold of Al. Stay put for a moment, and I'll get someone to bring a wheelchair."

Lillian did as she was told, and it was good to see color in her face again after warming up. Within a few minutes, two attendants helped her into a wheelchair and took her away. Priscilla parked the car and found the waiting room. Her stomach rumbled, and she realized she hadn't eaten since breakfast, and it was well past two o'clock. She rummaged through her purse and found enough change to buy a granola bar and a small bag of pretzels from the vending machine. Then she sat on a couch in the waiting room.

There was a cooking show on the television, which didn't help her rumbling stomach. She wasn't interested in the tabloid magazines either, but there was a book that drew her attention. It had been left on a coffee table with a pile of bookmarks next to it, so she assumed it was for marketing purposes, for visitors to read and consider buying.

She read the back cover first and then the introduction. It looked to be a locally published book about the sinking of the RMS *Republic* in 1909. It was written by Shawn Jackson, a local man. Priscilla didn't recognize the man's name or his picture on the back cover, but as she started to read, she became fascinated by the story.

Three years before the *Titanic*, another White Star luxury liner sank off the coast of Nantucket Island, which was not far from Martha's Vineyard. On January 23, 1909, a cargo ship carrying Italian immigrants to New York City became disoriented in dense fog and crashed into the RMS *Republic,* loaded with wealthy passengers headed to the Mediterranean. Most of the 1,500 passengers and crew were rescued, but six people lost their lives. The *Republic* sank fifty miles off Nantucket. All the baggage and cargo was lost, including a secret cache of rare gold coins intended for delivery to Czar Nicholas II. The American Eagle gold coins were estimated to be worth more than one billion dollars today.

Priscilla was drawn into the story, especially the efforts of those who'd searched for the wreck over the years until its discovery in the 1980s. Shawn Jackson owned the salvage rights, and he'd conducted a few dives, searching for valuables, but only turned up china and damaged bottles of wine and champagne. He was considering selling his rights to a second party as he wondered if the rumors of treasure had any validity to them.

Priscilla was deep in the book when the doors to the emergency area opened and a nurse strode out, approaching her.

"Are you Priscilla Grant?" the nurse asked.

Priscilla nodded.

"Lillian asked me to tell you that she's been taken back so they can set and cast her ankle. We're thankful our orthopedic doctor was on duty. It was a bad break. You can go home now. She's very thankful you brought her in."

"Oh, but shouldn't I stay?"

"No. Lillian told me to relay that her husband's on his way. She wants to thank you for all your help, though. She doesn't know what she would have done without you." The nurse reached into the pocket of her scrubs. "Oh, and one more thing. She asked me to give you her phone number, and she wants yours. She says she wants to find a way to thank you."

Priscilla found a piece of paper in her purse and wrote down her number for Lillian. "Tell her I'll be praying for her, and that I'll check on her in a few days."

"I'll do that." The nurse smiled and strode away.

Priscilla stood. It didn't feel right leaving like this, but she'd done all she could. Now that she had Lillian's number, she'd have a way to check on her.

She tucked the number into her pocket before she remembered it wasn't her jacket. She reached to pull it back out, embarrassed that she'd been wearing Gerald's jacket the whole time. It felt comfortable, just like Gary's had. As she grabbed the phone number, something else slipped out with it. It was a note card. She tried not to spy as she tucked it back away, but something caught her eye . . . her name.

There was a numbered list of three things:

1. Aunt Mary's surgery
2. New recruits
3. Priscilla's adjustment MV

MV. Martha's Vineyard.

She turned the card over. A scripture was written there. Philippines 4:6 (NIV): "Do not be anxious about anything, but in every situation, by prayer and petition, with thanksgiving, present your requests to God."

This must be Gerald's prayer list.

Emotion filled Priscilla's chest and crept up her throat. She tucked the note card back into Gerald's pocket and hurried to her car. She fumbled with her keys as she opened the door. Her fingers were trembling, and she wasn't sure why. Even though she appreciated the fact that Gerald was praying for her, something scared her about that too. How did he think of her? Only as a friend? She hoped so...didn't she? She didn't know how to feel if he thought of her any other way. It had only been a year since she lost Gary. She'd yet to get over the pain...Was there room in her heart for anything more than friendship?

Her heart felt broken and fractured, lying out on the ground most days. Did Gerald want to come to her rescue, sweeping her up and carrying her away?

Did she want that?

CHAPTER NINE

After arriving home, Priscilla took Jake for a short walk and then heated up a quick microwave meal. She'd planned on an uneventful week, but it had been anything but that. First there was the theft at the birthday party, and then her weak attempts at helping find the missing medal. Then today there was Lillian's injury and the prayer list she'd found in Gerald's pocket. She hadn't been able to shake either from her mind.

The only way she'd sleep tonight was if she thought about things other than Gerald. She had to turn her mind back to the missing medal. At least those thoughts could be productive, instead of spinning around in her head like a vortex of worries, concern, and also hope.

Thinking about the stolen medal, Priscilla got out a notebook and wrote down all she knew. First of all, she knew the medal was there at the beginning of the event because she'd seen it nestled in the display case. Then sometime during the party, it disappeared.

Why would someone steal it? The motivation seemed key to discovering who was behind the theft. She'd start with looking up how much a Congressional Gold Medal was worth. The answer came with a quick Internet search. Since 2006, it was illegal for unauthorized persons to wear, buy, sell, barter, trade, or manufacture "any decoration or medal authorized by Congress for the armed forces." She especially made a note of that wording. The medal was definitely created to honor those who served during a war.

After Priscilla wrote down those notes, she wrote another question. *Why would someone steal the medal if they couldn't sell it?* Then she made another note. *Black market?*

She chuckled to herself as she wrote that. They were in Martha's Vineyard. This wasn't New York or Bangalore. Still, just because Martha's Vineyard was small didn't mean it couldn't happen. Could there be a collector on the island or mainland who wanted the medal? It wasn't a medal that was mass produced, so it wouldn't be something that would be easy to find in an estate sale, especially if the families valued it as much as Deanie. So could the rarity of it be why it was stolen?

Turning back to her computer, Priscilla conducted a search to see if a nearby appraiser might be able to help her figure out if collectors with such an interest lived on the island. Someone might have simply stumbled on the medal, making it a theft of opportunity rather than planning. She found a few local appraisers and made a list.

As she continued to search, one name caused her to pause.

"Willow Gibson," she whispered, sitting up straighter in her chair. Excitement built in her chest. She'd been so bothered by how Andrew Wright had treated her that she'd nearly forgotten Deanie had mentioned Willow. That fact seemed even more important now that she knew Willow Gibson was an appraiser.

Priscilla paused, noting Willow was right here in Vineyard Haven. "Silver Willow Appraisals and Antiques on the island of Martha's Vineyard is a professional personal property appraiser with a reputation for expertise, integrity, service, and confidentiality," she read. She studied the photo of the woman with perfectly styled, shoulder-length blonde hair and a smile that hinted at both knowledge and interest in truly unique finds. "Willow Gibson, Appraiser, PCGS, NGC authorized dealer, ISA member." Priscilla looked up what ISA meant: International Society of Appraisers. Willow Gibson seemed like someone who would be worth talking to. What was the reason she'd wanted to talk to Deanie? Were her motives pure? All those letters after her name made her seem like she would be trustworthy.

If an appraiser truly were reputable, he or she wouldn't be involved in selling congressional medals on the black market. And if they weren't reputable, would they confess anything to her?

Priscilla wrote down all of Willow Gibson's information for when she had the chance to talk to her. She added Willow to her list of suspects, and then moved on. Who else would be interesting to talk to?

She immediately thought of Jedd, the reporter for the *Vineyard Gazette*. He was still one of only a handful of people who knew the medal would be donated ahead of time. He would have had time to make plans to steal it, but why would he do it? Maybe if he was trying to be the first to report a big story? That would be good motivation. And it was big. Didn't Rachel say it was on the national news? But would a reporter really fall that low in order to catch a big break? Priscilla hoped not.

The next person who came to mind was Carly. Priscilla couldn't shake all the strange security questions Carly continually asked. She also didn't understand why the young woman didn't give straightforward answers about what she was researching. Was Carly really who she said she was? Or was she trying to hide her true purpose? Could her motive be to steal important items from the historical museum? Was she using her security questions to create a smoke screen to distract from the fact she was the one stealing the items?

Finally, there was Andrew, Deanie's great-nephew. He certainly wasn't pleased when she'd shown up to have lunch with Deanie. He hadn't liked Priscilla talking to his aunt. But why? Priscilla tucked a strand of hair behind her ear and tried to consider the situation from his point of view. Maybe he thought she had something to do with the robbery. Or maybe there was something he was trying to hide. What had he thought about his aunt donating the medal? Did he have any say or choice in the situation?

Priscilla sat up straighter. What if that was it? What if Andrew hadn't been happy about his aunt donating the medal? Would he have stolen it to keep it in the family?

There was a lot to consider. There was a lot to talk to Mildred about. Would it be too presumptuous to ask Mildred if it would be all right for her to take her list to the police?

A knock at the door interrupted Priscilla's thoughts. Jake jumped up and trotted to the door, wagging his tail. It had to be someone her dog knew, but who?

Priscilla opened the door, and her heart leaped to see Gerald standing there. She took a step back. "Gerald, won't you come in?"

He pulled off his cap and stepped inside. "I hope I'm not bothering you. I wanted to check on Lillian, and…I wanted to see if you were finished with my jacket. It's a part of my uniform I really need to have."

Heat rose to her cheeks when she remembered the note card she'd found in the pocket. "Yes, of course. I'm sorry I forgot to give it to you when I got to the car. I was distracted by concern for Lillian."

He wasn't in uniform now and wore jeans and a thick green sweater. He looked like a fisherman, like anyone she'd see around town. It was a more human side of him—one she liked. She rushed to the coat hooks and pulled off the jacket, handing it to him. "I really appreciate you letting me use it. And your help with Lillian. You were right. She suffered a bad break. They rushed her back when I took her to the ER, and an hour later they came to tell me they were setting her ankle. I was going to call tomorrow to see how she was doing. I didn't want to bother her tonight."

"I'm glad you were there to help her."

"I'm glad you happened to be here too. There was no way I could have helped her to the car by myself."

"God works in wonderful ways, doesn't He? One of my coworkers was supposed to check on the lighthouse early in the morning. He got a flat tire, so I filled in. The only way you can explain something like that is God was watching out for Lillian."

Priscilla smiled. "I'll share that with her. I think she'd like to hear it."

There was an uncomfortable silence, and Priscilla considered asking him if he wanted to stay for a cup of decaf, but she couldn't bring herself to do it. The anniversary of Gary's death was just a few days away. She couldn't bring herself to spend time with another man, even if it was for something as innocent as coffee. Not when her heart seemed unsettled about what she wanted with Gerald.

Priscilla stepped toward the door and placed her hand on the doorknob. "Thank you for letting me use your jacket, and thank you for walking Jake too. It was a wonderful miracle that you were here."

She started to open the door, but Gerald had yet to move that direction. Instead, he cleared his throat.

"Listen, I was talking to Mildred—I saw her at the store the other day—and she mentioned how bothered you were by the missing medal. I was asking around, and I found out many military medals can be replaced. I have an 800 number, but Deanie would have to call. From what I could see online, I'm not sure if this includes Congressional Gold Medals. But it would be worth checking into."

Gerald reached into his jeans pocket and pulled out a slip of paper, handing it to her.

"Thank you. I hope to talk to Deanie soon. If I do, I'll let her know. That would be wonderful if it could be replaced."

Gerald lifted his eyebrow and narrowed his gaze. "You're say-ing that it would be wonderful, but the look on your face says otherwise. What's going on?"

She shrugged. "It's just that if it gets replaced, it's not quite the same, is it? I mean, that medal was the one handed to her by the House minority leader, a senator, and the Speaker of the House during the ceremony at the Capitol. You can replace what was lost, but that will never make up for what was taken. Does that make sense, or am I just being overly sentimental?"

Gerald released a sigh and tilted his head as if really thinking about her words. "You're a wise woman, you know that, Priscilla Grant? It's an honor to know you and to call you a friend. And I'm not the only one who thinks that. I know that Mildred, Deanie, and Lillian think that way too."

Warmth filled Priscilla's chest, and she stood and watched Gerald squat down and scratch Jake behind the ear. She didn't respond to his comment. She knew he didn't need her to.

And it's an honor to know you too, Captain, she wanted to say but didn't. The peace that had settled between them was enough. Besides, she didn't want to push their fledgling friendship too fast. She'd let Gerald know her growing feelings of friendship at the right time.

CHAPTER TEN

The pitter-patter of rain on the cottage's roof tugged Priscilla from her sleep. The peace that had filled her after Gerald left and as she'd drifted to sleep had abandoned her. Her eyes fluttered open, and she looked to the clock. It was just after five o'clock, the sun still hidden beneath the horizon where it would stay for a while, and an oppressive, melancholy feeling pressed her back into the mattress. Was it the questions about the missing medal that caused this discontentment? Caused this pensive sadness? Or was it something more?

She rolled over and flipped on the lamp on the nightstand. She tucked her hand under her cheek, and her eyes fell on the photo of Gary that she kept next to her clock. Was she feeling guilty because she'd had such a sweet conversation with Gerald last night? Should she feel guilty?

Then, just as the rain ran in sheets down the seaside cliffs beyond her home, Priscilla's memories drenched her mind. She remembered the day—a couple of weeks before Thanksgiving— when Gary had received the doctor's call that the test results weren't good and that he hadn't much longer to live. But they hadn't needed the phone call to tell them the treatment hadn't worked. She'd seen her strong, capable husband weakening by the day. And by Thanksgiving Day, he'd only been a shadow of himself. As he turned over the carving knife to Rachel, too weak to use it, it was clear that he wouldn't make it until Christmas. And then he passed just a few days after Thanksgiving. A year ago this month was the true beginning of the end of the life she'd once known.

Priscilla closed her eyes, trying to cope with it all. If she had a choice, she would keep the drapes closed and remain in bed all day. But she didn't have a choice. There was a Saturday tour scheduled. Strangers would be paying to come and see the lighthouse, and she had to get the yard in shape—not to mention it wouldn't do for someone to peek through a window and see her lounging in bed.

Still, Priscilla didn't even try to fight the emotions that tugged on her heart. She decided to get up and get ready for the day. Since it was still too early, and too dark and cold, to work on the yard, she put on one of Gary's favorite CDs and put all the angst into cleaning her cottage. Tears trickled down her cheeks as she swept and mopped. Then as she straightened items and dusted, she flipped her sadness on its head, and turned it to gratitude. Thanksgiving was coming, but she wouldn't wait. She'd start today.

"Thank You, God, for all the years I had with Gary," she prayed in a soft whisper as she loaded the last dishes in the dishwasher. "Thank You for the sweet, gentle rhythms of life on the farm. But just as I know that You prepared a place for me all those years in Kansas, I know You have a purpose for me here too. I came dreading the loneliness of living alone, so far from family, friends, and community, but You have surrounded me with family and friends in this new place. You've provided the beauty of creation just outside my window to remind me that You have provided beautiful things in this new life too. You've even given me a purpose, no matter how small. And even though it seems like a simple thing, Lord, help me to make a difference in someone's life today."

As she closed the dishwasher and ran it, she noticed the sun had risen. Rays of light stretched over the frothy Atlantic. She turned and spotted Jake sitting behind her in the center of the kitchen floor. His head was tilted, and he eyed her as if trying to figure why she was up so early and acting so strangely. Even when she went to the hook where she hung his leash, he didn't move, as if wanting to make sure she was all right.

"I'm fine, boy, but thank you for being concerned." She chuckled. "Now what about that walk?"

Thankfully the early morning rain had stopped by the time they stepped outside. Her tennis shoes sank into the muddy ground, but Priscilla refused to allow her thoughts to pull her down again. There was a time to mourn, of course, but she knew that Gary wouldn't want her to get stuck there.

A smile filled her face as she imagined him seeing her here now. Emotions fluttered in her gut with the knowledge that he would be so proud of her. He would have also told her not to give up until she found that medal. To Gary a replacement wouldn't be the answer, no matter how thoughtful Gerald had been to learn that was even an option.

Jake led the way down the trail to the beach. Priscilla didn't want to walk all the way to the ocean's edge, not feeling up to a long walk as the wind cut through her. Instead, they turned and headed back to the cottage. They were nearing home and Priscilla was lost in thoughts of those last days with Gary when she felt her pup tug on the leash. She looked up to see her cousins walking toward her. Joan's car was parked behind hers, but she hadn't noticed their arrival in her contemplation.

A basket swung from Joan's arm. The basket seemed nearly as large as the sparrow-like Joan. By her side, Trudy walked with bouncy steps. Her hair seemed to have an extra fluff to it today, and it was good to see that she was feeling better. Following behind them was Gail. Her hands were tucked in her pockets. Jake lunged forward with even more excitement when he saw her. Priscilla's guess was that she'd brought him a treat.

"What are the three of you doing here?" Priscilla asked as she approached.

"We brought a picnic breakfast from Candy's, and we thought you could use some help with yard work this morning. We haven't been around very much, and we know keeping this place up is a lot of work. We didn't want you to feel as if you've been abandoned." Trudy paused. She turned her palm upward and lifted it to the sky. "The only problem is this rain. Do you think it'll hold until we can get these leaves raked up?"

Tears rimmed Priscilla's eyes. "I hope so. That's really so wonderful of you."

"Many hands make light work." Gail smiled as she tucked wind-whipped hair behind her ears. "If we hurry, we'll have time to enjoy our breakfast before we need to scoot."

Priscilla walked with a new lightness to her step. "I don't think you need to worry. We'll have plenty of time to eat and chat before the tour arrives." She chuckled. "And even if the yard isn't pristine, I'm sure they'll understand."

As she tucked her arm inside Trudy's for the rest of the walk back to the cottage, Priscilla lifted her face to the rays of sun that dared to penetrate the clouds. She thanked God for sending family to help drive the loneliness away. No matter what else happened in her day, Priscilla's cousins had made her feel loved and appreciated. They had every right to continue with their busy lives, as they'd done for so many years before she returned to the island, but their growing friendship changed everything. They not only helped her today, but she had a feeling they would be there in the future as she faced the holidays in a new place without her husband by her side.

Working together, they finished the yard work quickly. Then they enjoyed a quick breakfast inside the cottage. As they cleaned up, Gail and Joan told Priscilla and Trudy about their shopping trip earlier in the month to the Boston Christmas Festival at the Seaport World Trade Center.

Gail clapped her hands together as she described it. "My favorite part was the Gingerbread House Competition. They were works of art! One was a gingerbread garden that looked like a scene from the original *Charlie and the Chocolate Factory*. I can't even imagine how many hours that took."

Joan nodded. "And all the proceeds for the competition went to help homeless families. Isn't that creative?" Then Joan reached into her oversized purse and pulled out two large gingerbread figures dressed as elves. She handed one to Trudy and the other to Priscilla. "And that's why we brought these back for you. We just haven't all been together until now to give them to you."

Priscilla gasped as she studied all the details. "This is too beautiful to eat!"

Gail brushed a strand of hair back from her forehead. "Yes, we figured you'd say that. That's why we decided to bring breakfast too, which you had no problem eating." She wrinkled her nose with a smile.

"That was delicious, thank you so much. And you really outdid yourself." Priscilla stood and moved to retrieve some plastic storage containers. "Here, let me help you pack everything back up to take with you."

"Oh, we're not going to take any of these pastries home. Enjoy them yourself. Or if you know anyone…"

Priscilla tapped her bottom lip. "Actually, I do know someone. Have you met Lillian Salisbury? She's an artist who lives here."

"I've seen her work." Joan turned to Trudy. "And wasn't there an article about her last year?"

Trudy nodded. "Oh yes, she has quite a following, especially in the UK, if you can imagine that."

Priscilla paused, leaning on the back of the kitchen chair. "I didn't know that, but I've seen her work. It's stunning. She injured herself on my property yesterday. She was painting the lighthouse and tripped and broke her ankle. I was thinking of picking up something in town for her, but if you don't mind, I'll take over these treats."

"Oh no, I don't mind at all. Feel free." Trudy helped her pack up all the leftover treats and then glanced at her watch. "But we must get going. We promised the church we were going to stop by and help them with their decorations for Sunday." She sighed. "And I'm not even going to mention that we'll have to redo them in a few weeks for Christmas."

Priscilla gave them all hugs goodbye. Her cousins had been gone just a few minutes when the white van pulled up with eighteen tourists—all women—for the tour. As they exited the tour bus, Priscilla overheard them telling the driver they were all part of a mystery writers' group and had come to the island for a plotting retreat. She smiled to herself. Was there really such a thing?

Priscilla knew she could just walk back into her cottage and shut the door behind her and no one would think anything of it. After all, her cottage was not part of the tour. But a nudging inside told her to stick around. If they were mystery writers, they most likely knew a thing or two about how to solve crimes. With a warm smile, Priscilla approached the group of women and introduced herself. "I happen to live here. Let me know if you have any questions about the place." Then her smile grew. "I haven't lived here long, but I can try to answer your questions."

While some of the women snapped photos of the lighthouse, the property, and the sea, a few of them approached Priscilla with eager looks, as if amazed she actually lived there.

One of the women, Priscilla discovered, was a woman named Kristi who was trying to write a novel set in a lighthouse. Priscilla listened as the young woman with long black hair talked about how she'd always been fascinated by lighthouses and the legends that surrounded them.

"I was researching this one." Kristi pointed to the lighthouse. "Built in 1852, and so interesting that it's been moved twice, due to erosion."

"Would you like to see inside the lighthouse?" Priscilla asked.

"Well, I've seen photos online," Kristi said. "But I'd love to see inside your cottage."

"Sure." Priscilla smiled. "It's housed the families of lighthouse workers for centuries. I'm not sure if you're writing a historical book, but many things are exactly the same as they were when I was a child. And my cousins told me that things haven't been changed much since my grandparents were first married."

Kristi's mouth opened, and her eyes widened. "Are you serious? I'd love to see inside. Do you mind a few of us looking around?"

Priscilla didn't know why she was being so generous today. She was usually fine with allowing the tour guide to do her own thing. But she had a feeling that interacting with these young women would actually help her stay out of the funk she'd felt earlier today.

She led them into the house, and the women spread into every corner, exclaiming over the hurricane lamps, the shelf of antique books, the simple design of the cottage, and the art.

"I can't believe that you really live here," a young redhead said, peering out of the kitchen window. "This view is amazing. It might be the best view on the East Coast."

"Then again, I'm not sure I'd want to live in Martha's Vineyard with all the robberies." Kristi pulled her sweater tighter around herself and shivered. "We read about the poor woman who lost her war medal. I could hardly sleep last night knowing that someone who did that was still here on the island. I mean, if someone would do something like that to a sweet old woman, what else are they capable of?"

Priscilla folded her arms across her chest. "Let me guess, a writer of murder mysteries perhaps?"

Laughter spilled from all of the women around her.

"Yes, she is," squealed a brunette with a bobbed haircut. "How did you know?"

"Oh, a good guess."

After that, Priscilla showed Kristi all the secret nooks and crannies around the place where items could be hidden or someone could hide. Kristi recorded notes into her smartphone and snapped dozens of photos. When they finished, she was already weaving a plot with her friends as they left the cottage and walked toward the lighthouse.

"You know," Kristi told Priscilla, "I think you gave me a wonderful idea of a twist for my plot. In my mystery, the things that are stolen aren't going to leave the cottage at all. Instead they'll be hidden by the person who's planning on buying the place. Who just happens to be the murderer too, of course."

Priscilla nodded. "That's clever. Be sure to write and tell me when the book is out…although I already know whodunit." She chuckled, leading them back down the path to the lighthouse.

After the tour of the exterior of the lighthouse was finished, Priscilla smiled and waved as the busload of writers drove away.

If only real-life mysteries could be figured out so easily, she thought with a sigh.

With the tour group gone, Priscilla had another mission for the day. She gathered up the treats her cousins had left and promised her pup they'd go for another walk once she returned. Then she strode to the car, thankful the clouds had cleared even more. The last thing she wanted was to get caught in a storm.

She'd texted Lillian after her cousins had left, asking if she could come by sometime during the day. Lillian had texted back her address with a few directions. Priscilla entered the address into the GPS app on her phone and saw it would take a good fifteen minutes to drive to Lillian's home on a part of the island Priscilla hadn't visited.

The drive into the country was beautiful and more rural than she expected. There were large fields, barns, and even livestock. If it wasn't for the aroma of saltwater in the air—and the tall masts of ships on the horizon—she could pretend she was back in Kansas.

Following the GPS's directions, Priscilla smiled when she reached Lillian's house and saw it was a cottage and hobby farm. She drove slowly down the dirt driveway, taking in the decorative front porch and the paved path that led to what looked like a large garden, now dormant for the winter months. The green shrubs that lined the front walkway were the only signs of growth and life. The other plants were just sticks and stubble, remnants of their former beauty.

The quaint place seemed like the perfect space for an artist. Gathering the treats, Priscilla walked to the house and knocked on the door and then heard a voice calling, telling her to come in. She opened the door and sucked in a breath. The inside was as bright and beautiful as she assumed the outside looked in the spring.

The floors were painted a dark gray, and the walls were white. White shelves lined the foyer, filled with baskets and trinkets. There were items salvaged from the sea, antiques, and a few paintings she recognized as being Lillian's. The pieces were artistically arranged, and even though there was a large number of items, the space didn't have a cluttered feeling.

"Come in, come in!" Lillian called.

Down the hall in the living room, Lillian was on the sofa. She lay reclined with her casted ankle propped on two pillows.

Priscilla hurried toward her. "I brought you some treats, but I should have called and asked if you needed anything else. I could have stopped at the store, the pharmacy—"

"Oh no," Lillian interrupted. "My husband has been a wonderful nurse." She laughed. "I suppose his practice of taking care of the livestock through the years has paid off. Just as long as he doesn't try to tag my ear." She giggled. "I'm not sure what I would have done without you yesterday. You were so helpful, and your friend was so kind. Is there more than friendship? I saw the way he looked at you."

Priscilla blushed. "What do you mean . . . the way he looked at me?"

"Oh, after he helped me in the car, Gerald turned and watched you approach with such tenderness in his eyes. Then he rushed forward to take my easel and other things. I'm sorry. I didn't mean to pry. I was just sure I saw a special spark there."

Priscilla lowered her gaze. She didn't know what to think. What to say. She supposed the best place to start was with the truth. She lifted her head and dared to meet Lillian's eyes.

"Gerald is a friend. To be honest, I'm not ready for anything more, and I most likely won't be for a while. I lost my husband last year, and…it's hard." She wiped away a tear that managed to escape. "I miss Gary so much."

"I'm so sorry." Lillian wrung her hands. "I didn't mean to bring up such a painful subject. Al's always telling me I should have been a gymnast. He says I'm super flexible since I'm always putting my foot in my mouth."

Priscilla waved her hand in the air as if shooing Lillian's words away. "Don't worry about it. You didn't know." She sighed. "Some days I'm doing better about learning to live without the man I was married to for so long, and some days are harder. Today is—was—one of those harder days. But God has been good to connect me with friends new and old."

After that they changed the subject, and Lillian pointed out more of her pieces of art from around the room. Then as Priscilla was preparing to leave, Lillian handed her a gift bag.

Priscilla opened it to find a small painting of Lillian's farm, of the meadow, and the gate.

"I painted it last year. I love the old gate, although Al threatens to replace it since the cows are always getting onto the road."

"I love it. It's beautiful. It looks like something that should hang in a gallery."

"That's sweet, but it's just simple. My way to let you know I consider you a true friend now. My home is yours anytime. My meadow, your meadow. My gate, your gate…"

Tears rimmed Priscilla's eyes as she thought of Kansas. Of her meadow and the gate that led to the road back home.

"Thank you, Lillian. I consider you a true friend too. Isn't that how God works? Because of a challenging situation, we know each other. So many times the hard things turn around to be good."

Lillian laughed. "What a way to bond."

Priscilla joined in, knowing she'd treasure the painting forever. "Yes, what a way to bond."

Then, as she was about to rise, Lillian grabbed her hand. "Priscilla, can I ask about your church?"

"Yes, of course."

"I used to go as a child. Al and I even went when we were first married, but over the years…" Her voice trailed off. "Well, it seems the stuff of earth has distracted us. When we still lived on the mainland, we didn't go to church because we spent most weekends here on the island. During those weekends, we wanted to take in as much of the land and sea as possible…Yet now that we're living here full-time, we really have no excuse." Lillian sighed. "Being around you, you're different than so many of my other friends. I noticed it right off when you invited me into your cottage that first day. I really noticed it yesterday when you helped me after my fall. Even during the emergency, there was a gentle calm about you. It's almost not of this world. Am I making any sense, or are these painkillers really messing with me?"

Priscilla chuckled softly. "I don't think it's the painkillers. Or at least I hope not." She paused for a moment and looked over Lillian's shoulder out the window to the fields and gardens that appeared dead now but in a matter of months would be alive with new growth.

"It reminds me of a sermon I heard from Pastor Lambert back in Kansas. He was talking about a scripture in John that says something like, unless a kernel of wheat falls to the ground and dies, it remains only one seed. But when it's broken open, it has a chance to grow—and then even to plant more seeds."

Tears rimmed Priscilla's eyes, and she brushed a stray tear away. "In the last year the stuff of this earth has really broken me open. My husband's death split my heart in two. And moving here has been wonderful but hard." She sighed. "Yet hearing you say that what you see inside me is not of this world encourages me to keep going. It's as if the brokenness of the last year is allowing more of Jesus to leak out." She took Lillian's hand in hers and winked. "And yes, He's not of this world."

Lillian was silent for a moment, and Priscilla saw tears rimming her eyes too. "I'd like to know the Bible like that," she finally said in a voice that wasn't more than a whisper. "Do you think I could go to church with you?"

Priscilla gave her hand a gentle squeeze. "Of course. When you start feeling better, give me a call . . ."

"No, I'm talking about tomorrow. Can you take me then?"

"But what about your ankle? Don't you think you should give yourself a week to rest?"

Lillian placed a hand over her heart. "I don't think I can wait a week. I really can't." She offered a humored grin. "Besides, I'm still on these painkillers, remember? As long as I'm careful, I'll be fine."

"All right." Priscilla released Lillian's hand and stood. "Do you think you can be ready by nine thirty? Sunday school starts at ten o'clock. That should give us enough time to get there and get you settled."

Lillian clapped her hands together. "Yes, I can be ready." A new light filled her eyes. "And I like what you said about the stuff of earth breaking us. I feel that...inside." She smiled. "And it's more than just my broken ankle. It's as if there's something changing within me. It's hard to explain."

Priscilla zipped up her jacket, preparing to step back out into the cold. "I understand. I remember when Jesus first started making waves in my heart too."

"Making waves." Lillian crossed her arms and pulled them tight against her. "I like that. I really like that."

CHAPTER ELEVEN

Priscilla drove away from Lillian's house, the warmth of a new friendship filling her with joy. It was easy to think her life was full and rich, but a few moments with Lillian reminded her of dear friends she'd left behind. She'd known when she uprooted from Kansas that there would be immense changes. What she hadn't anticipated was how long it took to go deep in friendships.

I need to put myself out there more. I need to reach out, not hide away in the cottage. So instead of returning home right away, Priscilla decided to spend some time around the town. After all, the sun was out.

As she walked around the small Vineyard Haven downtown, she tried to notice the people she passed. Maybe it was the reality of the anniversary of Gary's death or the newness of a fresh friendship that had her wanting to pay attention to the people around her.

She waved at Candy Lane as the baker arranged pastries in the window of her confectionery shop. Priscilla's mouth watered as Candy set up a sign for cinnamon scones. Those sounded too perfect to pass by, so she opened the door and entered the heavenly smelling bakery. Only a few of the dozen café tables were occupied. The time wasn't right for morning coffee or for afternoon tea, hitting in between.

"Candy, those scones look amazing. Can I have two to go and a cup of your coffee of the day?" Priscilla didn't know who she was going to share the second scone with, but she trusted that she'd find the right person at the right time.

"Sure." The woman left the window and collected two scones from the display case. After she boxed them in separate boxes, she poured a cup of coffee, leaving enough room for some cream. "Anything else today?"

"No thanks." A minute later, Priscilla continued her stroll through downtown, hands warming around the cup of coffee, the scones tucked in her oversized burgundy purse. The walk down the one-way Main Street was a familiar one, and one she wouldn't make much longer as the weather continued to worsen with winter. She passed Murdick's Fudge on Union, glad that she'd already treated herself to a scone. It made bypassing the shop's amazing aroma a bit easier.

After turning onto Manexit Road, she remembered her research. She paused. Willow Gibson's business was around here, Silver Willow Appraisals and Antiques. Since she was close, she might as well stop by and see if Willow would be interested in talking to her.

Priscilla again looked up the address on her phone. She couldn't see the business directly on Manexit Road, so she turned and walked down the narrow alley. She found it there, a storefront next to a nail shop.

The location for Willow Gibson's business wasn't quite what Priscilla had expected. There was no parking next to the building, requiring people to wrestle with street parking or to walk from lot parking. The white siding seemed fresh and was a nice complement to the darker roof, though the plate-glass window next to the door was in desperate need of a good cleaning.

Priscilla sincerely hoped the woman could help her untangle who on the island might be interested in obtaining the medal.

She paused in front of the door. Should she do this? Or should she accept that the medal was gone and order a replacement like Gerald suggested? Yet every time Priscilla thought she should give up her search, she'd see Deanie's face in her mind's eye. No, she couldn't give up...not while she had a viable line of inquiry. She had to do all she could to return the medal to Deanie. As each day passed, that outcome seemed less likely, which was exactly what propelled her to face Willow's door, armed with a cup of coffee and an extra scone.

"No time like the present."

Priscilla blew out a breath and then squared her shoulders. The photo on the website hadn't told her much more than that the woman she hoped to speak with looked to be about ten years younger than she was. She also had an impressive list of initials after her name, which Priscilla supposed were meant to communicate that Willow knew about coins and antiques. She opened the door and slipped into the business.

A tasteful antique couch, rich walnut wood offset by an old brocade in greens, sat against one wall. A worn but still beautiful Persian rug rested in front of it, with Tiffany lamps on small tables on either side. While the overall look was beautiful, Priscilla didn't want to walk across the antique rug and then settle on the elegant couch.

This was why, aside from a few family heirlooms, she didn't fill her home with antiques. She knew she would hesitate to actually use them. As much as she admired the elegant antique braided rug in her living room, she had to admit she preferred the comfortable feel of the bedroom, with its bright-toned rag rug set beneath the carved pineapple bedposts.

"Come in, come in!" A slightly heavyset woman with expertly styled blonde hair came from a hallway. "I'm Willow Gibson, the proprietor of this fine business. What brings you in today?"

Her effervescent presentation left Priscilla responding in kind. "I'm Priscilla Grant. It's so nice to meet you."

"Oh yes. The new owner of the Misty Harbor Lighthouse." The woman's smile got even broader. "Tell me you're ready to let someone in to appraise the furnishings in the cottage and the lighthouse. I've heard rumors you want to do something with the space, and you'll want a good appraisal to ensure you have the right level of insurance to protect against anything that could happen."

"That sounds like a good idea." And one she hadn't considered. But if she were to pursue turning the lighthouse into a museum—which is something this morning's visit with the writers had confirmed would be much appreciated by visitors— an appraisal would be a good idea, but not the reason she was there now. "Today I wondered if you could help me with another matter."

"I won't know until you tell me more." The woman gestured to a dark wood desk with matching chairs sitting in front of it. "These chairs were just refurbished and brought back. I'm still trying to assess whether there's sufficient padding to keep them here. We'll test them while we talk."

"Oh, but my coffee..."

Willow waved a hand. "It's fine. Just set it on the side table on the coaster. I trust you won't spill."

"I hope not." Priscilla placed her coffee on the small table and then cautiously edged onto one of the seats and found it surprisingly soft. "This is nice."

"I had them install an extra layer of padding. One simply wasn't enough." Willow sank onto the chair opposite then crossed her legs at the ankles with a Grace Kelly air. "Now, how can I help you? I'm quite curious, though I must tell you I have another appointment arriving in half an hour."

"That should be plenty of time." At least to get started. Priscilla took a breath and then explained the theft at the museum.

"Yes, I read about that. How does that relate to me?"

"I know next to nothing about antiques and collectibles. Can you explain the market for medals to me?"

Willow snorted, a sound that didn't match her carefully coifed image. She rested her palms on pants that had to be wool and then looked past Priscilla as if she gathered her thoughts. "I'll need to know a lot more. And you need to understand I deal primarily in antiques with just a smattering of coins. Being on such a small island, I need to be versatile in the services I provide. Still, my comfort leans toward antiques and collectibles."

"Did you have a personal interest in the medal?" The question came out abruptly, but it was the core issue.

"Whatever gave you that idea?"

"Deanie told me that you had contacted her and asked about the medal."

"I was curious to see it. It made such a splash when she received that award in 2010. Can you imagine that little woman traveling so far from the island at her age? I wanted to see it, and she was kind enough to let me satisfy my curiosity."

"Was it something you wanted to buy?"

Color began to climb Willow's neck. "Not at all. Like I said, I was curious. I'd never seen one and wanted to for a frame of reference. Sometimes being an appraiser is all about really understanding what you're seeing. Now that I've held one version of a Congressional Gold Medal, it will help if I'm asked to appraise one."

"I only saw it for a moment." Priscilla sighed, attempting to lighten the moment. "I wish I would have had time to take a closer look."

Willow's face softened. "It's a beautiful piece. And it was a well-deserved recognition for Deanie and her fellow WASPs. Can you imagine what they experienced?" She shook her head, but her hair didn't move. She must use Stick-to-It hair spray. "I enjoyed seeing it and hearing a story or two before Deanie got too tired to continue."

"Is this the kind of medal that collectors would be interested in obtaining?"

Willow cocked her eyebrow. "It doesn't make any difference to me as a licensed appraiser. Congressional Gold Medals cannot be sold."

Priscilla offered a knowing smile in return. "Not that you would ever deal in such a manner, but we both know that just because a Congressional Medal should not be sold doesn't mean that it doesn't happen. People do what they aren't supposed to do all the time."

"You're right. I would never do such a thing, but it's always possible another dealer would. However, there would be a very small market."

"How do you know that?"

"It's ridiculous to think there's a large number of people clamoring to own one. I'm not sure how many people even know that these medals were awarded. That medal has little to no value unless there's a wealthy collector who needs it to complete a set. Then its value can skyrocket."

"And maybe if a recipient, or a family member, is facing financial hardship?"

Willow smoothed a wrinkle in her pants. "You're right. If there was the right buyer who had a specific reason for wanting the medal and there was a recipient in need...then anything could happen." She shrugged. "I suppose some recipients would rather have a little money than the hunk of cheap metal."

"I'm certain Deanie wouldn't agree with that."

"A circumstance she made very clear. She barely let me see it before she vehemently denied she would ever sell." Her fingers fidgeting in her lap was the only hint that she found the conversation unsettling.

"If I wanted to sell the medal, how would I do that?"

"Find someone who is not as trustworthy as me who might have the contacts to find a buyer." Willow sighed. "That's the thing about collectors. There are always a few who will do whatever it takes to get a certain medal or coin. It's like an obsession to them. They must have the perfect item to finish their collection."

"And someone who runs an antique or appraisal shop on the island would be able to find those collectors?" Priscilla tried to keep the incredulity from her voice but didn't think she'd been successful. Martha's Vineyard was so small, though it was often filled with the wealthy.

"Yes. Those associations listed behind my name on my business card help me find and screen legitimate collectors as much as it helps customers screen me. But I didn't go to see Deanie because someone came to me wanting her medal."

Priscilla folded her hands on her lap, knowing the woman would not admit to otherwise, even if it were the truth. "That's good to know."

Willow forced a smile. "It's nice of you to care so much about helping Deanie. I'm sure she appreciates it since she's not able to do any of the legwork on her own. I'm sure it's nice for her to have a fan...or rather friend...like that. Do you have any other questions I can help answer for you? If not, it's almost time for my next appointment."

"Of course. Thank you for your time." Priscilla picked up her coffee and then remembered the extra treat she'd picked up. She placed her cup down again. "Oh, I have something for you." She took one of the boxes from her purse. "Candy Lane was putting these in the display case as I walked by—baked fresh this afternoon."

Willow's face brightened. She opened the box and licked her lips as she looked down at the treat. "Scones are my favorite. How did you know?" The tension in the room drifted away with the aroma of fresh-baked pastry.

"I didn't know, but they're one of my favorites too." Priscilla stood. "Thank you again for your time."

"I wish I could have been more help. Just remember, there wouldn't be a legitimate market for the medal. You have to under-stand that." Willow glanced at the door as a shadow passed the large window. "Someone like me with a reputation to maintain will stay far away from any transaction that might cause trouble. I take my commitment to act ethically and in the best interests of my clients very seriously."

"I'm sure you do." Priscilla extended her hand. "Thank you again. If I have other questions, do you mind if I contact you?"

Willow shook Priscilla's hand, expression firm yet hands slick with sweat. "If you have any other questions . . . I'm sure I'll have an answer. Even though it may not be one you want to hear."

"One last question. Were you at the birthday party? There were so many people there, I know I missed some."

"Oh no. I was at an estate sale for a client. One of the services I provide is to make sure people don't sell their things for less than they are actually worth." She smiled. "If the bids are too low, I 'buy' the item so we can sell it through another forum."

Priscilla thought about that a moment. "Is *that* actually ethical?" If the woman prided herself on her ethics, then she wanted to understand how she could justify a practice like that.

"Absolutely. There's a certain price threshold the item has to fail to hit before I'll intervene. Think of it as the reserve price." She smiled. "At some auctions, that price is very clear. At others the clients want to see what's possible without advertising the reserve."

"Would you ever sell a medal at an auction like that?"

"It depends. If it's a medal that's illegal to sell, then of course not. With others it would depend on if we thought that was the best way to get a good price. It all depends on the market, location, and item."

"Thank you." Even though she had all the information written down in her notebook, Priscilla took one of Willow's cards from the display at the edge of the desk. "This has been quite helpful."

Willow smiled. "I'm not sure how. I couldn't tell you much."

"When one knows as little as I did coming in, every detail is helpful."

But as Priscilla left the building and walked back to her car, she wondered what she had actually accomplished.

While Willow had answered her questions, she'd done it in such a way that Priscilla was left unconvinced that she was as uninterested in Deanie's medal as she wanted Priscilla to think.

She knew one thing: out of the few people she was still uncertain about, both Andrew Wright and Willow Gibson were at the top of the list.

CHAPTER TWELVE

Priscilla made it back to her car and was shocked to see that it was only two o'clock. She'd had breakfast with her cousins and given the thirty-minute tour of her cottage to writers. She'd visited Lillian and then interviewed Willow. Even with all that, she still had time to stop at the historical museum. Maybe she could get that much done every day if she got up at five o'clock in the morning.

Maybe stopping by the museum now meant that she would arrive after the curious tourists with questions about distant relatives who might have ties, however tenuous, to the island would have already moved on. Hopefully, she would catch Mildred before she left for her mother's cottage.

As she pulled in, she released a breath when she noted Mildred's and Carly's cars in the parking lot. Carly must really love her research.

As she climbed the wide, pale gray steps and crossed the old-fashioned porch to the museum's door, she noted the pots on each side of the door had mums sheltered inside them. They might not last long when the weather turned colder, but they were a pop of bright fall color for the moment.

She followed the front entryway to the kitchen, checking each room as she passed it. The lights were on, but the only noise came from the closing of something plastic. Must be the Keurig.

When Priscilla entered the kitchen, Carly stood over the Keurig looking as if she were praying for a good cup of really strong coffee. "Rough day?"

The young woman startled and turned toward her. Her hair lay in tousled dark waves around her shoulders, and she wore a chunky, pale blue turtleneck sweater and ripped jeans. Her mouth smoothed into a small smile when she spotted Priscilla. "Just more questions than answers. People tell me that's par for the course in adulting."

Priscilla laughed at the thought. "Yeah, adulting can be full of more questions than answers. Anything I can help with?"

"I don't think so."

"I've been told I have a good listening ear."

"Thanks." The young woman grimaced. "Unless you can do something about the security here, I don't know that there's much you can help me with."

Priscilla lifted her eyebrows. Hadn't Carly been talking about the same thing the last time she was here? Priscilla sat at the kitchen table. Was all her talk about security to distract from the fact that she might have taken the medal? She'd certainly had the opportunity on the evening of the birthday party if she were there, as Priscilla suspected.

The question Priscilla kept returning to was *why*? Why would Carly care about the medal? It didn't have much value, if any really, other than steep sentimental value for Deanie and possibly her family—which reminded Priscilla that she really needed to sit down with Andrew and find out whether he had taken the medal. If he would give her the time of day, that is.

"I don't know much about security. Never had much need for it on a Kansas farm."

"But now you live on the island. Surely you have security at the lighthouse."

"Don't think I need it."

Carly turned around and slammed a cupboard door shut. "What is it with people on this island and the crazy idea you don't need security?"

"There aren't that many of us who live here, and crime rates are low." Priscilla smiled to herself, remembering the response of the mystery writers earlier in the day.

"Until something you value is stolen."

"Is that what's happened? Has something been taken from you?"

"No." Carly blew out an breath then turned back around. "Well, maybe. There are items missing from this museum. It drives me crazy to think there might be more missing that I haven't discovered."

"We all know the medal is missing."

"No, I'm talking documents and maps." She picked up her mug of coffee then took a sip and made a face. "This is terrible!" She rummaged in the refrigerator then poured flavored creamer into her mug. She certainly was making herself at home at the museum and very familiar with areas that were usually off-limits to guests. Priscilla considered asking Carly about the maps that Mildred had discovered missing, but then changed her mind. She didn't know what to share with whom. Maybe it was better not to share what she knew with anyone except Mildred or the police.

Mildred wandered in dressed like a lady from the Civil War era. The red crosshatch on cream made a pleasant pattern on the long dress that had a slight bell to the skirt. She tugged off gloves as she walked to the coffeemaker. "I see you found what you needed."

Carly ignored the pointed look. "Caffeine will help."

"It usually does." Mildred popped the old cartridge out and inserted one claiming to make Donut Shop coffee.

"I'm surprised you're here since you were headed to your mother's today," Priscilla said to her.

Mildred yawned. "I spent last night at Mom's, then my sister offered to spend the morning and early afternoon with her so I could get back here. I'm so worried about finding the medal and other lost items, I could hardly settle in at Mom's. I'll head back there in an hour or so."

"I'm glad your sister could help."

"Me too." Mildred's skirt belled out as her body nodded.

Priscilla wanted to ask if a hoop hid under the skirt but had a feeling she already knew. "Carly was telling me some items are missing."

"Not missing. Misplaced." Mildred sighed. "We try to keep an organized research area, but I can't promise every person who comes in to conduct research is as conscientious as you are, Carly. You know that."

"But there's so much you could do to make sure the narratives and journals are protected. Do you have a single security camera around this place? I sure haven't seen any."

Mildred poured water into the reservoir then stood over the coffeemaker as if counting to ten. Then she turned to Carly with a tense smile. "As I've told you, we have a security camera, and it wouldn't be well placed if everyone knew where it was."

"You have a security camera?" Priscilla's mind started to race with the information they might be able to get off of it related to the medal. "Where is it?"

"It's at the front door. Aimed to let us know if someone breaks in."

"Or supposedly let them know if someone leaves with a bulging bag." Carly set her coffee down and sank into a chair at the table. "That's what I've been trying to tell you. No one is going to walk out with a bag stuffed with loose papers and crumbling journals. That's not how it's done."

"How is it done then?" Mildred's voice was shrill. "I've run this museum successfully for a number of years. It still exists because I've found a way to attract corporate support. This museum maintains an important part of our island and state's heritage and history. I do not take that lightly, and I do not need a young upstart from the big city to tell me how to protect my collection." She turned toward the door, skirts swaying. "If you'll excuse me, I find I need to get away."

Priscilla would have smiled at the way her friend's language changed to match the time period she was dressed for except her distress was clear. Carly's face had leeched of color, and Priscilla reached across the table to touch the young woman's arm. "I'm sorry for Mildred. She's under a lot of stress. She doesn't usually behave this way."

"Seems I push all her buttons."

"Security issues do." Priscilla frowned but tried not to worry about Mildred. "Why are you so concerned?"

"There are journals and maps *missing*."

"Why don't you believe they're simply misplaced?"

"Because they were here a month ago when I came up for a quick trip to check the museum's resources and see if they were worth a closer look. My boss wouldn't have paid for an extended stay if he wasn't as convinced as I was that there was gold in the items."

"What kind of gold?"

"Not real gold." Carly's laugh was nervous. "Just that they had the information he needs for his project."

Priscilla watched the young woman as silence settled between them, heavy and uncomfortable. The girl fidgeted but didn't say anything, holding her coffee mug close to her mouth as if ready to take a sip at any moment.

"You should be glad to hear that the museum has a security camera."

Carly nodded. "But having just one camera is a joke." She took a final sip from the mug and then stood to place it in the sink. "I'm going to see if any missing items are in the archives. Wish me luck."

The young woman headed out, her head down as if afraid Priscilla would try to ask her something else. Priscilla stayed at the table as she plotted the best way to approach Mildred. Her friend had been so defensive, there must be something to Carly's concerns. The best way to attack it was probably to ask if anyone had checked the security camera footage after the birthday party.

She stood and wandered through the rooms of the historical museum. When she entered the dining room, she found Mildred dusting the platters displayed in a china hutch. "You all right?"

Mildred stopped with the feather duster in the air. "I am."

"Can you show me where the camera is?"

"Not you too."

"I had a thought. Maybe what's on the camera will give us some idea what happened with the medal."

"How do you think that the footage from one camera is going to help? The police looked at it and didn't think it was important."

"Let's look at it and see."

"I'll have to get someone to help me. The technology is a bit beyond me."

"If you could, that would be great." Priscilla had a feeling the footage would show something they could use. And right now anything was better than the nothing she was working with.

CHAPTER THIRTEEN

Priscilla had an unsettled feeling as she left the East Shore Historical Museum. It had been four days since someone stole the medal, yet she couldn't tell Deanie she'd accomplished anything toward finding it. She felt like her work had been a wash, vain and without effect. She really wanted to be the one to take the medal to Vineyard Village and return it to her friend. She wanted to see the smile of relief when it was returned.

At least she could run back by Candy Lane's and pick up some cranberry muffins for her Sunday school group. The coffee klatch loved having something a little sweet as they discussed the scriptures. It was her week, and the treats from Candy Lane Confectionery would be the perfect pre-Thanksgiving delight. As she entered the nautically themed store for the second time, she saw that half of the café-style tables along the right-hand side of the shop were filled with tourists. A few other tables had locals seated around them.

The line at the counter was several deep as Candy ran around filling a box with delicacies. Priscilla took her place, then glanced around when she heard a slightly familiar bass voice. Andrew Wright was seated at one of the four-toppers, a mug of coffee and a plate bare of all but a few crumbs in front of him. He was focused on a newspaper that lay in front of him while he carried on a conversation with someone on his earpiece. How did his generation multitask so effortlessly?

"This never would have happened if my aunt had kept the medal like I asked." He rubbed his face, and she noted the bags under his eyes. "I don't think she understood how much I wanted it."

He paused as if listening intently, nodding occasionally. "Yeah, there were so many people there, anyone could have snagged it. Security is a sieve in that museum. It wouldn't take much at all to walk in with a briefcase or purse and walk out with something as small as that medal. You wouldn't even need anything to carry it in, thanks to its size."

He nodded again then ran his hands through his hair. "Aunt Deanie? She's acting as if her faith will make everything all right. Does she really think trusting God and praying hard will bring it back? I just want to tell her she should have listened to me. Think of what I could have done with that medal."

Priscilla's mind raced as she listened to the conversation. Why was he talking so openly inside a busy bakery? Was he trying to throw off suspicion by making it sound like anyone could have snagged the medal? Did he get so upset with his aunt that he took the medal? She didn't want to think he would, yet he looked frustrated enough that it didn't seem impossible. She'd known families that had been divided over the distribution of seemingly small items in an estate. It would be easy to make the argument that something as rare as a Congressional Gold Medal could be a very big deal.

"I've spent so much time helping her out, and she repays me by giving away the one thing of hers I actually wanted. It isn't right." His voice had slowly gained in volume as he spoke. But then he must have realized his error because he looked around the small shop and abruptly stopped talking. He froze, and his eyes got bigger when he spotted Priscilla.

She waved her fingers at him as she decided how to respond. Maybe she could let him think she hadn't heard a thing.

"Great talking to you, but I've got to go." Just like that Andrew ripped off his earpiece and pasted on a smile. "Mrs. Grant."

"Hello, Andrew. I didn't expect to find you here." She stayed in line but turned his direction.

"A guy's got to get his coffee, no matter the time of day." He patted a small pastry box on the seat next to him. "Also picked up a treat for Aunt Deanie. She has quite the sweet tooth. I figure at her age she should be able to eat anything she likes." His attitude was completely different than it had been yesterday. What had changed?

"Makes sense to me." Priscilla chatted with him another minute. It was as if she'd discovered Dr. Jekyll after yesterday's Mr. Hyde. She then inched forward as the line snaked ahead. She considered taking a moment to step out of line and talk to him, since talking to him was on her list, but this wasn't the time or the place. Andrew might not care who overheard his conversation about his aunt's missing medal, but she was more discreet than that.

What had all of that been about?

Then again, was this her opportunity? What were the odds that the one person she still wanted to talk to happened to be right here? And she could talk to him and still be discreet.

Priscilla glanced over her shoulder. Andrew still sat at the small table, flipping through his newspaper. Had he gotten off the phone because he realized she was standing nearby? It sure seemed so. She smiled at him and stepped from the line. It would be a while before she got to the front, so she might as well talk to him a bit. "Do you mind if I join you?"

He glanced around as if hoping she were talking to someone else. "I suppose for a moment. Candy will likely ask for my table back if the line doesn't get shorter."

"I'll be glad to use it." She tugged out a chair and dropped into it. "Feels good to rest a minute."

"Busy day?" His question was polite, his expression interested.

"A full day, indeed. I think I've overdone it, since I woke at five. I'm weary now." She smiled at him as she traced a pattern on the table. "Coffee seemed like a good idea."

"Some would argue it's rarely a good idea so late in the afternoon. Though caffeine doesn't affect my sleep."

She nodded. "Most days I would agree, but not today." She leaned into the table. "How's your aunt doing?"

"Aunt Deanie? She's fine. Why?"

"Oh, I'm just concerned. I feel guilty in a way."

"Why?" His look was confused. "It's not like you stole it."

"True." Priscilla shrugged and tried to explain why she felt such ownership. "I'd really hoped someone would have located the medal by now."

"It may be long gone by now." He watched her from under squinted brows. "I'm not sure there's much we can do. It's too late."

"I don't want to believe that." Priscilla blew out a breath and noted that the line to order was getting shorter. "I'll keep asking questions." She shrugged. "It doesn't hurt to do that. Maybe we'll learn something. And maybe we'll find it after all."

"Please don't say that." Andrew's voice turned sharp, causing her to jump. "That's what made me so upset yesterday when I saw you at Vineyard Village. I could tell by the joy on my aunt's face that she believed you would find her medal for her. She's one hundred years old, and she doesn't need to have anyone filling her head with false hope."

"Is that what you think? That by asking around about the medal, I'm offering false hope?"

"Isn't that what you're doing? I believe I've heard you say twice now you would find the medal for her." He softened his scowl. "You shouldn't make promises you can't keep."

Priscilla folded her hands and placed them on the table. She considered telling Andrew that the joy Deanie had found hadn't come from her promises at all. Instead it came from the faith that, no matter what happened, God had everything in His hands. Yet she didn't say it. Deanie had said it many times already. Andrew had even repeated it on the phone.

Instead Priscilla swallowed down the emotion she felt building within her. "You're right . . . I'm trying hard, but it's not something I should promise." She leaned forward. "I'm sorry if I've made things difficult for you. But how is your aunt really?"

"She's fine other than she really doesn't care that the museum didn't take proper care to secure her irreplaceable memorabilia." He shrugged. "She won't consider suing. Doesn't think it's important and says she'll be dead before anything could happen anyway."

Priscilla couldn't help but laugh at his put-out tone. "She's probably right. Your great-aunt seems very content with her life. I've really enjoyed our conversations."

"She's been charmed."

"Do you have any ideas about who might have stolen the medal?"

"Anyone who was there."

"No thoughts at all?"

"Look, I love my aunt, but the party got out of hand. For all I know, she told everyone at her home that she was making the donation. She says she didn't, but how can we know for sure? From there, there's no way to know exactly who could have come for the purpose of stealing the medal instead of celebrating Aunt Deanie. The proverbial cat was out of the bag."

Priscilla studied him, but he didn't look up from where his phone rested on the table. His shoulders slumped in sadness, and she realized he wasn't Mr. Hyde at all. Instead, he was a man who was trying to do what he could to protect someone he loved very much. The silence grew, but he didn't budge, and Priscilla wondered if there was a reason why Andrew was so protective. Did her great-nephew know something he hadn't revealed?

"Okay. Surely your great-aunt has friends who might have spread the word. But maybe she also had enemies..." Priscilla let her voice trail off.

"She's a hundred years old. I'm sure she has some of both. Doesn't mean they could do anything about it. Her friends are mostly as elderly as she is."

"So maybe the next step would be to figure out if there was anyone who did this not because they wanted the medal, but simply because they wanted to hurt your aunt. But who?"

He lifted his gaze, and his eyes met hers. Sadness and worry conflicted within his pensive look. "I really can't help you."

She settled back and studied him, and from what she could see, he was telling the truth. "At least she had a great party. One she enjoyed."

"Until the last minutes." He sighed and took a swig of his coffee before glancing at his watch. "She was pleased, and I'm glad for that. I've got to get to an appointment. Have a great evening."

Before she could say anything, Andrew stood, picked up the treat he'd bought for his aunt, and practically sprinted out of the shop. The door slammed shut behind him, having narrowly missed hitting a woman walking with her toddler along the sidewalk. Had her questions really rattled him that much? They didn't warrant a bolt from the shop. She took a moment to think about what Andrew had said before standing, and then Priscilla stood herself. She might as well get the pastries she'd come for.

She waited while Candy rang up a large order. As soon as that was completed, Priscilla walked to the display case and smiled.

Candy's answering smile lit up the place. "Already back for more?"

Priscilla patted her purse. "I've already gifted one scone, and I'm saving mine for dessert. But yes, I'm back for more."

Candy chuckled. "Just the type of customer I like. What else can I get you today?"

"Do you have a dozen of your cranberry muffins left?"

"Those have been popular today. How about a mix of cranberry, blueberry, and banana nut? I can add a couple of blueberry that are gluten free."

"That sounds perfect." The muffins were large enough she could cut them in half or even quarters so people could sample the selection. "It's my turn to provide the treats for my Sunday school class."

"That's great! Thanks for coming back to get them here."

"Sure. Your baked goods are the best."

Candy brushed her hands along her apron before slipping them into gloves. She was soon filling a pastry box with her creations, and Priscilla had her add an extra for tomorrow's breakfast.

"Do you know Andrew Wright?" Priscilla dared to ask the baker.

Candy paused and looked up from the box. "Seemed like you knew him."

"Not really. I only met him at Deanie Spangler's birthday party."

"He's pretty devoted to her. She's fortunate to have him."

"Does she have money he's hoping to inherit?" The words sounded crass, but she had to wonder what prompted his devotion.

"Not that I know of. Deanie's always had enough, but I'm not sure there's much extra when you live to be her age. Back in her working days, no one expected to live to see a hundred."

"Crazy to think that'll be us someday."

The women shared a chuckle as Candy finished filling the box. She paused after she put the lid on. "He's a good boy. Knows she doesn't have any other family around here so has taken it upon himself to be that for her, even though they aren't close relations." A soft smile touched her face. "I love watching him with her when he brings her here." She walked to the cash register and rang up Priscilla's order.

"Thanks for the perspective. Like I said, he seems devoted. I'm glad she has someone to dote on her."

"Me too."

"It seems as if your day has been busy. I hope you can put your feet up tonight."

"I like it this way." Candy looked around the store with a hint of pride in her sparkling eyes. "I love sharing my baking with everyone. It helps keep the calories off my hips." She winked at Priscilla. "But yes, putting my feet up will be good."

When she finally got home, the sun had set and Priscilla was looking forward to putting up her own feet. As she settled in for the night, she thought about the many conversations she'd had throughout this very long day. Joan, Gail, and Trudy. Kristi. Lillian. Carly and Mildred. Willow. Andrew. Candy. "No one could accuse me of hiding out in my cottage today," she said to Jake as she let him out.

When she boiled down the day's discoveries, she decided everything came down to the fundamental question: Why would someone steal Deanie's medal? What were they trying to accomplish? Was there any way that Priscilla could find the medal before it was too late to stop them?

And had Andrew Wright been correct...had she been hurting Deanie more than helping by promising she'd do all she could to bring back the award?

CHAPTER FOURTEEN

Sunday morning dawned overcast and with the hint of rain in the air. The melancholy continued to linger over Priscilla as she lay in bed. Jake walked to the bed and nuzzled his nose under her hand. When she didn't move, he did it again and whined. When he sat back, he wore his most pathetic puppy dog expression.

She couldn't help laughing, even as she longed to cocoon in the bed and not come out for several days. Even the knowledge that she had to get the muffins to Sunday school didn't help her to move. She needed a few minutes to process what was happening deep inside her heart. The grief and sadness over missing Gary had faded through the day yesterday as she'd kept herself busy. But now in the quiet morning—without people or clues to draw away her thoughts—the emotions were back in full force.

The gray sky did little to help her mood, and if she hadn't promised to take treats to Sunday school, she would have spent the morning in bed.

Then Jake whimpered, and she threw back the covers.

"All right, boy. I'll let you out." Even with the covers thrown from her shoulders, she still lay there, unmotivated to move.

Jake grabbed the quilt and tugged it down. His determination urged her to climb from her warm bed, and reluctantly she swung her legs over the side and pushed to a sitting position.

"I'm up." She might have been physically up, but she knew it would take more to find a zone where her spirits matched. "I guess I didn't expect it to be this hard."

She should have. She'd read books on grieving and had thought she understood the process. Still, this month of anniversaries was pushing her toward a place she didn't want to go, one she'd have to fight. "Let's get you out. I'll make some English breakfast tea, and then we'll go for a walk—just a short one. I have friends who are waiting for those muffins."

Jake's ears perked up at his favorite word, and she stood before stepping into her slippers and then pulling on her robe. A few moments later she'd let Jake out and had a kettle warming on the stove. She opened the refrigerator and stared inside. She should eat. She knew that. But nothing appealed to her—not even the muffins—and the idea of forcing food wasn't something she was willing to think about.

She closed the refrigerator and poured boiling water over a tea bag. Then she headed back to her bedroom to change while it steeped. After pulling on comfy yoga pants and a long-sleeved shirt plus a hooded zip-up jacket, she put the lid on her mug and grabbed Jake's leash. Once he was hooked to the leash, he danced impatiently as she pulled the door shut.

Priscilla lifted her face to the sky and waited a minute. *Lord, I need You today.*

While she knew she needed Him every day, today would require an extra measure of His grace. She let Jake lead where he willed, seeing waves fall over each other in their race to the shore. Some driftwood had been carried to shore in the night. One especially large branch was laced with seaweed and foam, a tangle of rustic and delicate beauty. A lone ray of sunlight shifted through the clouds to light the foam with an iridescent shimmer.

That was life.

It was a mix of hard and easy. Beautiful and ugly. Moments packed with joy and others overwhelmed with grief. It was in the mix of the two that God's beauty shone through the cracks, turning it all into a beautiful piece of art that reflected His hand guiding through all things.

Father, show me Your beauty in the mess of life.

As the walk continued, she let her mind wander through a kaleidoscope of memories. The first time she saw Gary and was captured by his strong, capable hands and broad shoulders. The first date when he took her to the wrong restaurant, and they laughed about the missing reservation. The sight of his face when she stepped into the church's aisle in her wedding gown and walked toward him. The birth of their daughter, Rachel. The sunsets on the farm. So many beautiful and crystalline memories that took on new meaning when the doctor looked across the desk at them and said the terrible words that were forever imprinted in her mind: pancreatic cancer.

The weeks after that had been a swift blur.

Then there was his funeral, the graveside service. The days trying to decide what to do. The letter telling her about the lighthouse.

A sand dollar caught her attention. She stooped down to pick it up, but as she touched it, a side crumbled away. It was like the perfection of her life with Gary. Oh, they'd had their moments, but the word *cancer* had caused their life together to crumble.

She lifted her gaze from the fragile sand dollar to the horizon. At the point where the ocean kissed the sky, some brave soul had a sailboat. She'd begun to feel that kind of freedom in fits and starts now that her life was settling into a rhythm here. Gary would always lay claim to a large piece of her heart, but life was becoming good again. Today she'd continue to sink into creating good memories with new friends and allow herself to recognize the beauty of life here on Martha's Vineyard.

Jake whined at her as he tugged against the leash. Poor boy always preferred to run free. He whined again, and she allowed him to lead her back toward the cottage and his kibble.

Once inside, Priscilla quickly got ready for church. Even with dragging her feet and the walk along the shore, she could still make it to Sunday school on time. It wasn't quite nine fifteen. Then Priscilla's eyes widened as she remembered she'd promised her new friend Lillian a ride to church.

Priscilla texted Lillian to let her know she was on her way. Then, collecting her Bible and the pastry box of muffins, she hurried to her car. If she didn't leave right now, she'd be late collecting Lillian, which would then mean the treats would be late for those in her Sunday school class. That was the kind of outcome she couldn't allow, not when Gerald would tease her.

She climbed into her SUV, and after starting it immediately hit the button to warm the seats. By the time she reached Lillian's house, she was toasty warm. Hopefully that warmth would linger while she collected Lillian. Her new friend was waiting by the door, her leg propped on a blue-and-white chintz ottoman. She had a pair of crutches and her purse. Al was nowhere to be seen.

Lillian's hair had been twisted up into a soft bun on the back of her head, and a few soft curls fell around her face. "Thanks for coming to get me."

"My pleasure." Priscilla waited as Lillian levered to her feet and grabbed her crutches. "My car's right out front, and it won't take long to arrive at Faith Fellowship. I think you'll enjoy the class. The muffins alone will make it worth it."

Lillian laughed and patted Priscilla's arm. "I appreciate you taking me with you. I really have been thinking about what you said...about the wheat, that is. And I'm sure I'll enjoy meeting your friends and worshipping with you."

After a careful trek across the porch and down the stairs, Lillian settled into the SUV. "The seats are warm."

"One of my little splurges."

"One you'll enjoy this winter."

"I definitely did in Kansas." It only took a couple of miles to reach the simple church. The white columns that framed the verandas made a pretty impression. With the weather so brisk, people weren't lingering on the porches to catch up like they would during warmer weather. Instead, they hurried inside and did their greeting at the back of the sanctuary.

Lillian twisted in her seat. "Those old oaks are beautiful."

"I know. Every time I see them, I wish I had my camera. There's something gripping about the image of their twisted branches curling in and out of each other. It's even more stark with most of them bare of leaves."

Soon they were inside and saying hello to friends. Lillian warmly engaged with each of them, almost as if she were testing them to see if they were new friend material too. Priscilla watched, delighted to see her friends embrace Lillian. She was thankful that Mildred seemed more at peace today, maybe because Carly wasn't tagging along, asking questions.

The three walked together down the hallway to the fellowship hall where the adult Sunday school class met. Priscilla found a tray and knife for the muffins while Mildred chatted with Lillian. As Mildred and Lillian arranged the treats on the tray, Priscilla got a pot of coffee and an electric kettle of water ready for the drinks to accompany the muffins. Then she pulled a handful of small creamers from her bag.

"I thought people might enjoy something fun to mix with the coffee."

"You know I'll take mine black." Gerald's deep voice caused Priscilla's heart to pick up its pace, but she refused to show him any reaction.

"And you'll have it thick enough that a spoon can stand up without assistance." Mildred tsked. "I don't know how you can drink it that way."

"And I'll never understand how you believe it's all right to abuse coffee by marring its perfect flavor."

Priscilla laughed at his dramatic flair. "The Coast Guard must have ruined you on coffee, or you use a much nicer coffee bean."

"Wouldn't you like to know." He winked at her, and she felt warm at the easy way they could banter. Heat rose to her cheeks when she remembered her name on his list of prayer requests, but she quickly pushed those thoughts away. Instead, she thought back to how her heart would skip an extra beat whenever her husband entered the room, even after all those years of marriage. She so missed these kinds of conversations with Gary.

The thought made her pause as she watched her friends grab a muffin or two and then a mug of their favorite hot drink. She still missed Gary in the depths of her core. You couldn't spend thirty-four years with someone and not miss the many ways they intersected with your life. When that person was a spouse, you couldn't separate them from you—not in a few months or a year. And she didn't want to. Yet as she watched Gerald interacting with Lillian, saw the kind way he crouched down to talk to her so she could be comfortable without standing, she saw reflections of Gary, and her heart stirred even as she wanted to back far away. She wasn't ready for anything with someone else.

She'd known widows who were so lonely they immediately started seeking someone else they could love. That wasn't her. She was building a new life separate from the constant reminders of Gary. The struggle was, she had been married much longer than she'd been single. She'd forgotten what it was like. Now it was time to learn about herself again. To dig deep and see who she was all alone.

But when she was ready to start thinking about that possibility again, someone like Gerald would be the type of person she'd be willing to open up her heart for.

Tilly Snyder walked over, a frown on her face. The petite dynamo ran the Colonial Inn and Restaurant and had more energy than people half her age, not that anyone was sure what that was. "Are these muffins from Candy Lane?"

Priscilla gulped, remembering the long-standing humming-bird cake feud between the two women and hoping it hadn't spilled over to pastries. "It is. It was my week to bring treats, and I ran out of time to make something." Not that she'd really wanted to when someone else could bake scrumptious items while keeping the mess out of her house.

Mildred strolled over in a pair of wool pants and a pretty fall sweater. "Well, I think they're wonderful. And you know you do too, Tilly. I saw you sample each kind."

"It's opposition research."

Mildred laughed as the woman walked away. "Don't worry about her. She lets the pastry wars go a little too far."

"Thanks. I really was hitting the easy button for today."

"We all need that button at different times." Mildred forked off a small piece of muffin and then sighed as she chewed it.

"I hope you didn't stay up too late working at the museum. But I must ask, did you notice anything else missing?"

This time Mildred's sigh wasn't grounded in the contentment of a yummy muffin. "Carly insists there are items missing. If I'm honest, I can't be sure they're actually missing. It's just as likely they're misplaced."

"Why do you say that?"

"You've seen how hectic it can get. I don't always get the time I'd like in between helping people to make sure everything is put back in place immediately. I'm still looking for those folders and old ledgers from shipping routes." She set the plate on the table. "I really need to find an intern or two who can help me get caught up. I just never seem to have the time."

"I bet Carly would be delighted to help."

"Except I'd probably need to pay her, and I'm not convinced yet that she's not creating more of a problem."

"I think she's sincere." There had to be a way to confirm the young woman's story so that the cloud of suspicion could be proven or cleared. Priscilla would need to check on that. Maybe asking Carly a few questions, drilling down into the type of research she was doing and for whom, could help—and not let her wiggle out of it this time.

From there Priscilla could do some checking to confirm what Carly had noticed was missing. She could spend time at the museum helping Mildred go through the piles. It couldn't be terribly hard to put things back in order.

From the pinched look on her face, Mildred didn't agree Carly was completely sincere. Maybe she too was starting to wonder why Carly always evaded their questions. "I'm convinced she's bringing big-city problems here. I'm sure things disappear in Boston more often. They have so much more in their collections, it would be hard to notice, making it easier to slip things out." Mildred waved a hand in the air as if batting the concerns away. "Even with the little bit of disorganization, I know she's creating a problem. I didn't used to think this, but after all that happened last week..." She let her voice trail off.

"You're certain?"

"Yes." The word was hard and quick.

"How about I come help you get some of those items filed, and then you can prove she's bringing big-city issues here."

"If you have time, I'll take it. It would be nice to get everything back in its place."

"I'd be glad to help too." Lillian looked interested as she adjusted her foot on the chair in front of her. "I'm not good for much right now, but I can help file."

Mildred frowned. "I wouldn't want to put you out."

"Not at all. I would enjoy getting out and doing something while this silly ankle heals." She turned to Priscilla. "Just tell me when you plan to go, and if you could pick me up, I'd love to help."

"Sounds great." Priscilla could sense the woman's need to do something. The thought of being trapped for days with a foot propped was terrible. Besides, she'd love spending more time with her new friend. She turned back to Mildred. "We'll plan on coming to the museum tomorrow or Tuesday. Just let me check my calendar at home."

"All right." While her tone was reluctant, Mildred's eyes were warm and her posture less tense. Maybe, despite her words, she feared that there was truth to Carly's concerns. If Priscilla could help prove or disprove those concerns, it would be a great use of her time.

She glanced over and noticed Gerald watching her with a grin. When their gazes connected, he shook his head and smiled larger. *You found another puzzle.* His mouthed words affirmed what she knew. She'd been working on it all week, and he found it amusing.

"Are you having fun?" His rich voice covered her with warmth.

"Yes, actually I am." She'd never imagined her move to the island would bring with it so many puzzles and mysteries, but she enjoyed them. "But I won't really have fun until that medal is recovered and returned to Deanie."

"If anyone can find it, I'm sure you're that person." His quiet confidence bolstered her.

She wanted to tell him she'd been working all week and had yet to make significant inroads, but instead she settled into his approval. "If you were to take a medal, where would you hide it?"

"You're presupposing I have experience hiding things." She arched a brow at him, and he laughed. "All right, with a little imagination, I'd keep it close for a month or two and then try to find someone who could sell it for me. I doubt anyone around here would value it intrinsically like Deanie would. So that means they'd want to sell."

"That's the problem. Selling a Congressional Medal of Honor is illegal, so if someone were to sell it, there would be no record of the transaction. And if someone stole it and doesn't intend to sell it, then why do they want it?" Priscilla shrugged. "It's part of the mystery."

"I have no doubt you'll untangle it."

She wished she had Gerald's certainty. The longer she considered who had taken the medal, the more unsure she was she'd locate it. Her heart's desire was to find it and return it to Deanie so the precious woman would know it was recovered and could then give it back to the museum or possibly keep it if Andrew persuaded her to do that.

"You're worried about Deanie." His statement made her feel like he could read her mind.

"Yes, I am." She didn't want him to think her crazy or overbearing, but she knew just how old the woman was. "She's not guaranteed another day."

"None of us are, Priscilla." His words were gentle. "Besides, she looked very well at the birthday party. Looked like she could live another year or two."

"She did. There was something about all that attention that she loved."

"We all love being seen." He patted her hand as their Sunday school teacher made his way to the center of the room. "You'll do everything you can. The rest is up to God."

His words were filled with truth, but she couldn't escape the reality that Deanie was one hundred years old. She needed to find that medal before it was too late. Despite Gerald's assurances, Deanie wasn't guaranteed another day.

CHAPTER FIFTEEN

The ringing of her phone, which was charging on her bedside table, woke Priscilla Monday morning. Her dreams had been peaceful, and as she struggled to find the phone, she wished for a little more time to sleep in that peace. It kept ringing, and finally her fingers gripped around the pesky alarm. She slid a finger across the screen, squinting at it while she wished for the good ol' days of a telephone that you simply picked up to answer.

"Hello?"

"Good morning, Priscilla. I hope I didn't wake you."

Priscilla glanced at the clock radio on the bedside table. Eight o'clock. She'd slept a little later than normal but nothing crazy. "It's all right, Lillian. I thought I'd pick you up at 9:45."

"That's fine. I just wanted you to know there are scrumptious muffins here for breakfast. I set one aside for you."

"That's so thoughtful. Thank you."

"No problem. A friend dropped them off, and there are more than enough for Al and me to enjoy." Lillian paused, and Priscilla wondered what she needed to talk about. "I just wanted to say thanks for reaching out to me so well. I know you don't have to, and I appreciate your friendship more than I can tell you."

Priscilla sat and pushed against the headboard, feeling the pineapple posts tap the wall behind her. "Thank you, Lillian. That means a lot to me. I'm really enjoying getting to know you. I'll see you in a couple of hours." She quickly called Mildred and left a message that she and Lillian would be at the museum at ten ready to work. "We are going to make progress today."

She believed they would. If nothing else, they would end some of the speculation about whether items were disappearing or simply not filed correctly and misplaced. That would be significant progress.

After selecting an outfit from her antique tallboy dresser and getting ready for the day, she placed a quick call to Willow Gibson. "Good morning. I have a quick question, if you don't mind."

"Want to know who can corroborate my alibi?" There was a side of sarcasm in her voice, but Priscilla ignored it.

"Actually, I wondered if anyone had contacted you about the medal since we talked."

"Other than the police? No."

"I just got to thinking that someone might not know of your integrity and offer to sell it to you."

"I suppose that could happen, but no one in their right mind would bring the medal to me. I know it's stolen. Even if I hadn't talked to you and the police, it's been in the media. The first thing I would do is alert the police." She paused, and when she started speaking again, her voice was a touch friendlier. "I really wish I could help you, but I've heard nothing."

"Are there dealer groups you're in where someone might post about the medal?"

"Possibly."

"Would you monitor those for us? Let me know if anyone posts about wanting to sell it?"

"I can do that, but I really think it's too soon. Something like this won't come up for sale until time has passed."

"How long?"

"Usually a couple of years or more."

"Unless the person stole it for money."

"Then they will be disappointed. I doubt it would sell for more than a couple thousand dollars."

An hour later when she arrived at the cottage to collect Lillian, Priscilla thought she had a plan for the morning. Lillian asked her to carry a large tin, and she was quick to oblige. After she got Lillian settled in the car and set the tin between them, she ran through her thoughts. "Mildred is stressed because she has items that need to be filed. Until they are, she can't confirm whether anything else is missing."

"As long as I have a place that I can prop up my ankle, I should be able to tackle that piece of her stress."

"That would be great. I thought I'd have her explain her registration system and how someone could abuse that system." She kept her eyes on the road and slowed for a four-way stop. "A young woman who has been doing extensive research with the historical documents keeps bringing up security concerns, and I think it's bothering Mildred more than she'll admit to not have a clear answer to give."

"It's part of her job to know, and she doesn't." Lillian shifted against the car's seat. "I can understand how uncomfortable that would make her."

"Me too." And that's why they would be at the museum the moment it opened. Priscilla drove the car into the parking lot, thinking through everything that needed to happen.

As she parked, another thought hit her. What if the medal had never left the museum?

She thought back to the group of writers who'd visited her cottage, and she remembered the conversation she'd had with that young woman named Kristi. In Kristi's novel she planned to have the thief hide all the stolen items in the nooks and crannies around the lighthouse and cottage, with plans to purchase the property and its hidden treasures later. What if the person who stole the medal on Tuesday night hadn't left the building with it after all? What if the person had just tucked it away in an inconspicuous place for it to be claimed later when there weren't so many people around and when the police weren't searching everyone who left the building?

It seemed so simple. They'd all assumed that the medal had been stolen, but what if they were wrong? What if the medal was tucked into a corner someplace?

The police had searched bags and jackets as they interviewed people and found nothing.

Lillian opened her car door and eased outside on her crutches. A moment later she leaned back in. "Are you coming? I can send someone to help you if you need it." Her tone was saucy, as if she might be getting a little weary of people helping her.

"Sorry. An idea hit me."

"I hope it didn't hit too hard. That would hurt."

Priscilla laughed as she opened her door and collected the tin as well as her purse. "It wasn't that brilliant. Just something to try."

Mildred was waiting in the kitchen, watching a cup fill with coffee. She turned to them with a small smile. "Thanks for giving up part of your day again."

"I'm glad for the excuse to get off my couch." Lillian adjusted her crutches. "It'll be nice to kick these crutches to the curb and regain some independence. I'll go crazy if I spend another uninterrupted day at home without the ability to tackle the projects taunting me."

"I have a few here you can do."

"That's what I was counting on."

Priscilla grabbed two mugs. "Would you like some coffee, Lillian?"

"Sure. It'll be nice with the muffins."

"Muffins?" Mildred glanced toward Lillian. "Is that what's in the tin?"

"Yes. Someone from your church brought them over last night so I'd have them first thing this morning. They're scrumptious, but I really don't want to expand like a boat. Please take at least one."

The ladies settled at the table with their mugs of steaming coffee and the muffins, chatting while they ate. As soon as they were done, Mildred led the way up to the low-ceilinged second floor. A couple of library-style tables were situated in the middle of the room, each with several chairs. File cabinets lined the walls, and several display cases sat against the far wall.

"This space used to be three small bedrooms, but we renovated it into the archives. My office is tucked behind the displays. Next to it is a locked room where we store the most precious items that could be destroyed if mishandled. All of this space is temperature and humidity controlled to help preserve the documents and items." Mildred went on to explain the organizational system. "Those cabinets have the family records, those over there have records on the island's buildings, and old newspaper microfiche fill those three cabinets."

Lillian leaned against the table as if she needed to take some pressure off her foot. "How can I best help?"

"I thought she might help with the filing you need." Priscilla hoped Lillian wouldn't be offended by her suggestion, but she also knew that, despite assurances her ankle was getting better, Lillian needed to baby it just a little while longer.

"That should work." Mildred led the way to her desk, where several boxes overflowing with files and documents teetered on the edge, looking one breath away from sliding onto the floor in an avalanche of paper. "Have a seat." As soon as Lillian sat, Mildred handed her gloves and then explained her system. "So most of this should be filed by family name. If you have any questions, let me know."

"I'll try not to interrupt you too much."

"I'd rather you do that than guess." Mildred softened her words with a shrug. "After all, Priscilla and I will be up here too. It'll be a simple matter to answer any questions."

"Thank you." Lillian straightened her cardigan and then shifted against the chair. "I think I've got enough to get started."

Priscilla walked with Mildred to a library table. "I had an idea on the way here."

"Yes?"

"What if the medal never left the museum?"

"You mean someone took it, but really just moved it?"

"Exactly. The police searched people before they left. While they weren't invasive, I really think they would have found the medal if someone had it in a bag or a jacket pocket."

"Maybe." Mildred paused, and her eyes moved as she considered the idea. "But the medal is so small, it would be easy to tuck somewhere. It's not like the police patted everyone down."

"But I think they would have noticed a medal of that thickness in someone's clothing."

"I'm not sure, but it's worth checking. Where would you like to start looking?"

Priscilla thought about the layout of the museum and where people had been the night of Deanie's party. The downstairs rooms had been crowded, which could make it tricky to hide something without someone seeing. "Did anyone come up here?"

"They weren't supposed to, but that doesn't mean someone couldn't have slipped up the stairs without us noticing. Normally I can hear anyone who's moving across the floors, but there were too many people here that night to distinguish sounds. I was too busy serving as hostess to watch everyone and didn't have anyone posted or anything blocking access to the stairs." She sighed. "I'll do that next time."

"It would be a good idea, considering all the treasures you have up here."

"It's easy to forget someone might want to steal things."

Someone clomped up the stairs, and a minute later Carly stepped into the archives. "Good morning." Her nose crinkled like a curious rabbit as she glanced around. "What are you all doing up here?"

Lillian piped up from her post. "I'm helping organize these papers."

"I could help." Carly smiled at Mildred. "I'm so glad you're doing something about this. If you're right, I could find the documents I'm looking for while I help."

"What are you researching?" Priscilla's curiosity got the best of her. "You've been here quite a few days."

"About a week this trip. But I enjoy the area. It's no problem to spend time on the island."

Why was she sidestepping the question again? Priscilla smiled but pushed again. "It must be something really interesting."

"I suppose. But I was a history major, so being lost in a place like this is my idea of a wonderful day. There are so many stories to uncover and tell."

"She's researching shipwrecks and their effects on families." Mildred rolled her eyes as if to communicate she couldn't understand why Carly didn't just say it. "There were plenty of those in this area."

"I saw an interesting book on that last week when I took Lillian to the hospital."

"You were such a saint." Lillian stood and, using one crutch, brought a stack of papers to them as heat traveled into Priscilla's cheeks from her words.

"I am not."

"You were when I needed someone." She hobbled to Mildred and showed her the stack. "I think these go in the family files. Do you want to double-check and then show me which cabinets those are?"

"Sure." Mildred flipped through the stack, easing a couple of items from the pile and setting them to the side on the table. "These actually go in the ship files. Let me show you where the rest of these go. I'll just be a minute, Priscilla."

"No problem. I'll think of where we should start." But first she had a few questions to ask Carly.

CHAPTER SIXTEEN

I'm so glad you're doing a search here." Carly's words rushed over each other as if she were determined to forestall any questions Priscilla could ask.

"It seems like the next step." Priscilla steeled herself, determined to push through Carly's elusiveness. "Carly, I appreciate that you might not be able to share everything you're doing for your boss, but I really think it would help us all if you shared more about what you're *really* doing."

"What do you mean?" Carly's back straightened, and she pivoted slightly like she was ready to bolt downstairs.

"The more you insist on being coy, the more I wonder if you know something about where the medal is."

"Mrs. Grant, I didn't have anything to do with that. In fact, I'm the one who's been yelling the alert since I got here that this place is vulnerable to thieves." She squared her shoulders and lowered her voice after a quick glance at Mildred, who was working nearby with Lillian. "It would take zero skills to walk out of here with documents and journals. Throw in a few photos for good measure. Maybe a map or two as well. It's a simple matter to do that, thanks to the open nature of this." She marched over to a box on the edge of a file cabinet. "Did you know this is how Mildred tracks who's here?" She grabbed a binder from the box and thrust it at Priscilla. "This is it."

Priscilla opened the binder and found it was full of pages of log-in information. Mildred left her work to come to Priscilla's side and look over her shoulder. Priscilla scanned the page and then turned to the next several. There were gaps and places where someone had signed in but failed to sign out. "What's your system, Mildred?"

"Most of the time I'm with the people who are doing research. I ask them to sign in and out and to leave a note about what they came to find. Some do, some don't. It really shouldn't matter, since I can check the computer database to see what people have searched for. That gives me an idea of who's looking at what."

"But it's a completely voluntary process." Carly sounded exasperated and ready to abandon her quest. "There's no security, no real way to gauge what people came here to look for and evaluate whether they actually found what they wanted. It's an honor system, like leaving a dollar when you take a doughnut."

"There's never been a problem." Mildred's words were as sharp as a sword's point.

"Until last week." Priscilla whispered the words, but Carly and Mildred both whipped their attention to her.

"Exactly." Carly nodded. "And there have been several items I've looked for that, according to your records, should be here but aren't. It's entirely possible they walked out the door."

"Really! It's equally possible they are in those piles on that desk." Mildred threw her hands in the air. "I've about had enough of the hounding. I run this museum largely on my own. That means every system isn't perfect, but it's worked for years. The medal's theft doesn't negate my years of work. Look for the medal or go home."

Priscilla took a breath and slowly released it, hoping some of the tension in the air would dissipate at the same time. "I'm sorry, Mildred, I really want to help you. I hate that the medal is gone, and I'll keep doing everything I can to help you and Deanie reclaim it."

"I'll help Lillian." Carly skirted around Mildred and hurried to Lillian's side, sliding a chair closer as she went. She sat and waited for Lillian to explain things to her.

"I think I've got this system figured out," Lillian told Carly.

The two put their heads together over the piles, and Priscilla had a feeling it wouldn't take them long to make significant progress. Before Mildred could get distracted by her frustration with Carly and her questions, Priscilla tried to pull her attention back to a hunt in the museum for the medal.

"What do you think about starting up here since we can't be sure whether anyone came upstairs?" Staying here would also mean Mildred was close while Lillian continued to settle into her organizing task. "Should we start with the file cabinets closest to the stairs?"

"It's as good a place as any I suppose." She sighed. "I really think this is a waste of time."

"Maybe, but I'll feel better if we take the time to check here for the medal." Priscilla was still determined to do everything in her power to find the medal and return it to Deanie. Searching the museum was a small-time commitment toward that effort. She moved to the file cabinets. "Okay then. I'll take this first one."

Mildred tucked a strand of gray hair that had slipped out of her bun behind her ear. "Might as well start there. If nothing else, it'll get you ladies to leave me alone about security here."

"You know we're only concerned for you."

"*Hmph.* Tell yourself that all you like."

"I think it's a great idea." Carly walked by on her way to the ship files. "The medal is so small, it would be easy to take it from the display and tuck it somewhere and then come back to retrieve it after the excitement is over."

"Then you'll be disappointed to know the museum wasn't very busy last week after the theft." Mildred yanked a drawer open.

"Maybe it just rolled out of the case." Priscilla knew she was grasping at straws but felt the need to explore all possibilities.

"That's not possible, and you know it. The medal did not roll away or get knocked out of the case."

"I'll admit it's unlikely, which is why we'll search as thoroughly as we can." Priscilla opened the top drawer and methodically flipped through the files, feeling along the sides and bottom for the medal. She repeated the search through each drawer in that cabinet and then through the cabinets around it.

After an hour, she moved to looking behind the cabinets and then stood with her hands on her hips looking around. Mildred had gone downstairs when a family entered the museum a while earlier. "I'm going to head downstairs."

Lillian and Carly barely looked up from the piles that were steadily shrinking thanks to their focused efforts.

"We'll be fine here." Lillian smiled her way. "Thanks again for bringing me. This has been a nice way to spend the morning, doing something useful."

Priscilla chuckled as she headed downstairs. Lillian was a woman after her own heart, with her ability to dig in and work hard with a cheerful attitude. Now she needed to keep her own spirits up as she reentered Mildred's orbit. That woman was a stress ball, and Priscilla wanted to help her without absorbing the attitude. Mildred was a strong woman with a dominating spirit. Priscilla knew she'd be fine in the end, as long as the three of them "helping" didn't push her over the edge. But first they had to find the medal and get back on steady footing.

A small family stood at the counter, and Mildred was pointing out the different rooms and handing a scavenger hunt form to the children. "See if you can find the items listed on here. There's at least one item in each room."

The kids seemed less than thrilled, but the mom smiled. "This is great. Thank you."

Other than the family, the museum looked empty. Priscilla approached Mildred. "Ready to have me search the rooms down here?"

"You should wait until these people leave."

Priscilla glanced at her watch and noted it was approaching noon. "How about I make sure I stay out of the rooms they're in?"

"All right." Mildred frowned, but then the front door opened and a middle-aged man entered, a messenger bag slung over his shoulder. "Good morning."

Seeing that as her chance, Priscilla slipped into the parlor. The 1812 room was stiff and formal, and neither couch looked overly comfortable. One had scrolled, wooden arms with a butter-colored fabric but thin padding. Across a red-toned Oriental rug sat a narrow red-striped couch with thin, spindly legs. Priscilla eyed the couch warily, doubtful it could hold even her modest weight without collapsing. Small wing chairs flanked a fireplace topped with a painted mantle. A small grandfather clock was posted in a corner. As she studied the room, Priscilla decided it wouldn't take much time to search it. She started by running her hands along the crevices of the couches and got down to peek beneath them. She pulled up the corners of the rug then turned her attention to the chairs and mantle. Finally she examined as much of the clock as she could access. About that time the family wandered into the room, so she moved to the pantry.

The butler's pantry almost overwhelmed her. There were so many cabinets and drawers, she'd need to be methodical in her search pattern or it would be easy to miss the medal tucked away in one of them. She took a deep breath and then pushed it out as she approached the first set of drawers on her left. Slowly, she worked her way around the long, narrow room until she'd opened all the drawers. Most were empty, and the rest held a few kitchen utensils. It didn't take long to eliminate them. After that she started on the left again and worked her way around, this time focusing on the upper cabinets. When she found nothing in those, she stretched her lower back, trying to ease its dull ache.

"Are you about ready for lunch?"

Mildred's words startled her, and Priscilla turned to see her friend standing in the doorway. "I didn't hear you."

"I gathered that." Mildred waved at the room. "Find anything?"

"Not yet." And a part of her had really thought she'd find the medal here. There were so many nooks and crannies to slip something into. "I suppose I should check on Lillian."

"Carly said she would grab lunch for us. She's headed to the Nautilus Café to pick up sandwiches."

Priscilla's stomach growled, and she pressed her hand against it. "That would be great. Does she need money?"

"I took care of it. Seems the least I could do since you're doing all of this work." She straightened the button-down shirtwaist that topped her floor-length skirt.

"Thank you for that." Priscilla looked around the narrow room again. "I don't suppose you have a loose floorboard anywhere."

"All over, but I doubt anyone would have been able to pry one up while the museum was filled with partygoers."

Priscilla nodded. "I know you're right. Two more rooms plus the kitchen to check."

"No one who was a guest entered the kitchen."

"That we know of. I'll try to go through the dining room before Carly gets back with the food." She knew the dining room wasn't a very likely hiding place, given that it was the most popu-lated room the night of the party. Still, she wanted to be thorough and deliberate. Twenty minutes later, she was beginning to wonder if her idea had been a good one after all.

What if important documents and artifacts really were being stolen from the museum? Did their disappearing have any connection to Deanie's medal? Were they wasting their time searching the museum for it?

What to do? Where to look?

CHAPTER SEVENTEEN

The front door opened, and Carly pushed through it holding a couple of to-go bags in one hand and a drink carrier in the other. Priscilla hurried toward her, unsure how to best assist her.

"Can I help you with that?"

"If you could take the bags, I'd appreciate it."

Priscilla did as the girl asked. "We can set these in the kitchen on the table and eat there."

"I didn't realize I'd ordered so much food." Carly set the drinks on the table and then rotated her wrists. "Should we take it upstairs to make it easier for Lillian?"

"I'm on my way down." Lillian's voice floated down the stairs, accompanied by a hiccupping step-hop. A minute later she slowly made her way into the kitchen on her crutches, Mildred a step behind.

"I wasn't sure whether to go in front of or behind you, Lillian." Mildred pulled out a chair for Lillian then moved to the counter where she grabbed the napkin holder and put it on the table. "Should I say grace?"

The women sat, and Mildred bowed her head. "Lord, thank You for this meal and for the women around this table. If it's Your will, would You help us find the medal or learn what happened to it? Thank You for Your provision. Amen."

Carly handed out the Styrofoam containers. Priscilla opened hers to find a roast beef and Swiss sandwich, a bag of kettle chips, a scoop of coleslaw, and a wrapped dill pickle. "This is perfect."

Carly smiled, and her shoulders relaxed. "I'm glad. I wasn't 100 percent sure what you all would want, so I went with the platters."

Lillian took a bite of her coleslaw. "This is delicious. I'm afraid my eyes were beginning to cross after looking at the documents for so long. It was harder than I anticipated to decipher some of the handwriting."

"I know." Mildred unwrapped her pickle. "You'd think it would get easier, but every time I get in the files, I find something that's almost impossible to read either because of age or handwriting. Context becomes critical in those times."

"So what's next?" Carly pulled open her chip bag. "Is there anything I can do to help?"

Priscilla considered her question as she met Mildred's gaze. Her friend shrugged. Maybe she was finally warming to the young woman. If so, Carly should have gone for lunch days earlier. "I'm only halfway through the dining room. I could use help in there. Even though it's not the largest space, there are all kinds of nooks and crannies."

"I can do that." Then the girl looked guiltily at Lillian. "That is, if you don't need me."

Lillian took a quick sip of her Diet Coke. "We've made so much progress, I bet I can wrap up in the next hour or so. This was the break I needed."

They relaxed and enjoyed the lunch for another thirty minutes before cleaning up and getting back to work. An older couple entered about that time, and Mildred went to show them the details in the parlor that interested them. Her voice drifted to the dining room, and Priscilla half-listened as she explained to Carly where she had left off. "I'll finish the drawers and lower cabinets if you want to check the higher ones."

"I can do that." Carly moved into the interior of the room and started as far away from Priscilla as the small room allowed.

"Did you find anything interesting when you were upstairs?"

"There was such a random assortment of papers, and they were interesting in their own way." Carly closed one upper cabinet door and opened the one next to it. "How big is the medal again?"

Priscilla made the shape with her hand. "About like this."

"Okay."

"So what stood out to you from what you found?"

"I did find one of the diaries I was looking for." Carly shut the door. "Mildred was right in that instance. It simply hadn't been put back in its place."

"Maybe you'll find the others too."

"I hope so, but some of the maps are probably gone."

"What kind of maps are you looking for?"

"Related to old sea routes." She stood on tiptoe to reach into another cupboard. "I didn't realize how many potential hiding places this room held."

"Until you start looking, it's not obvious." Priscilla asked a few more questions, but Carly was hesitant to expand on her work.

"It's really not something I can discuss. I had to sign a nondisclosure agreement. I can't risk my boss learning that I told you about it." She closed another cabinet. "This job is going to pay for my books next semester."

"Are you in school now?"

"No, I had to take the time off to earn money. I try to work a semester, go to school a semester." She shrugged, but Priscilla could see the pain in her eyes. "My parents want me to be independent and don't approve of my career choice."

"Why?"

"They insist there's no gainful employment in writing. Guess my mom should have tried a little harder to keep me from reading all the time."

Priscilla's heart went out to the young woman. "One thing I've learned in a lifetime of walking with God is that He tends to make a way for us to follow the callings He has for us. It's not always a straight line, but it's His path."

"I wouldn't mind mine being a bit straighter." Carly straightened her posture and forced a smile. "It'll all work out, and I'm doing interesting work in the meantime. I certainly won't graduate without experience."

"I love your positive outlook." Priscilla looked through another drawer. "It will help you find your way."

They sank back into silence as they worked through the rest of the room. When they finished their search, Carly went to check on Lillian while Priscilla went to find Mildred. She had questions that only Mildred could answer.

Mildred was sitting behind the desk making a notation on her desk calendar. She finished it and then looked up. "What can I help you with?"

"Carly and I finished looking through the dining room. If it's in there, it was hidden very well." Priscilla sighed. "There aren't too many more places to look."

"I'm afraid we have to accept it's simply gone."

"I'm not quite ready to do that yet." Priscilla leaned a hip against the wall as she watched Mildred. Her friend looked so tense and strained that she was as determined to find the medal to help Mildred as she was to return it to Deanie. Both women needed it to be found and returned to its proper place. "I'm wondering if maybe we should approach this from another angle. Carly is pretty sure some artifacts have been stolen from the museum—" She held up her hand when Mildred opened her mouth to protest."—And I'm not saying she's right. I'm just saying maybe we could try to determine who was researching the files that are missing. Can you tell me more about the archive log?"

Mildred quirked an eyebrow at her. "What do you want to know about it? It's a pretty basic log."

"I only had a quick glance at it earlier, but it seemed that not everyone signs in and out. What's the protocol?"

"Anyone who wants to do research upstairs has to fill in their information in the book. I don't ask for much information, just their name and what they're researching."

"But not everyone signs out."

"True, and I can't guarantee that everyone who comes in fills it out when they arrive either. It's not like there are four of me. I'm restricted in how many places I can be at once." Mildred leaned back, her frustration clear in her crossed arms protecting her stomach.

"I know. You do a lot." Priscilla used her best placating tone. "Maybe we should look at the last few weeks. That would help us recreate who's been here and maybe prompt a memory about someone who didn't sign in."

"Fine, we can do that."

The two women went upstairs, and Mildred set the log on the table. "Okay, let's get started."

Lillian hobbled over. "Anything I can help with?"

"Not yet." Priscilla sank onto the chair next to Mildred. "We're just going to go through the log to see who's been here in the last few weeks."

"We've got our Nancy Drew hats on." Mildred cracked a smile, and Priscilla felt some of her tension leave as she caught it. Mildred ran a finger down the list. "These are the regulars."

"Is there anyone who should be on the list and isn't?" Priscilla wanted a way to make Mildred take this seriously. Why wasn't her friend more concerned about the lack of security? Carly met her gaze from across the table.

Priscilla nodded. "There had to be more visitors to the archives in the last few weeks than those listed on these two pages."

Mildred shook her head as her finger continued to run down the list. "It's not like the summertime right now. Then we could have dozens of people a week. Right now we have far fewer visitors."

"What types of research are people doing when they come?"

Mildred glanced at Carly. "Some are doing specific event research like our friend there." She sighed. "Others are doing genealogy research. Their topics and purposes are as varied as the people who come."

Priscilla sank against the hard back of the chair. What else could they do? "I wish there was more security footage."

"Someday I'll add more cameras, but it hasn't been in the budget." Mildred sighed. "But even if we'd had more cameras, what if none of them were pointed at the display case? It only takes a couple of seconds to take something and stick it in your pocket. If we couldn't capture those couple of seconds, what good are a hundred cameras pointed at everything else?"

"Still, I wish I could see that footage."

Mildred pushed the log back and stared at Priscilla. "The police have already checked the footage. It only captured video of the entrance. Like I said, we'll add more cameras as we have money. Right now my budgetary priority has to be acquiring more materials for the collection."

"But those materials won't be kept secure." Carly didn't try to hide her eye roll.

Priscilla tried to steer the conversation back to the camera. "Did you check about getting access to the security footage?"

"The police made a copy. And my tech guy showed me how to access it." Mildred pushed back from the table. "I can pull it up for you."

"Thanks." Before she followed Mildred downstairs, Priscilla took out her phone and snapped a photo of the two sign-in pages. She would study them more closely later. Unfortunately, she didn't think they would be much help. After all, what self-respecting thief would sign his name and then list the documents he was about to steal?

"You can sit here." Mildred got up then turned toward the door as a family with a couple of tweens entered. The kids looked surly, like the museum was the last place they wanted to be. "You should be able to watch all the video from here while I help this family. You can get my attention if you need anything."

"Thanks." Priscilla settled in the chair that Mildred had abandoned. It looked like Mildred had pulled up a site that didn't have much visible other than a grainy video. Priscilla noted the time stamp and the number of people milling in the museum. She hit Play and let the video scroll at a fast speed. There wasn't much to see at first. The door opened and shut on a steady stream of visitors. But as the time neared the announcement that the medal had disappeared, Priscilla made special note of who was leaving.

There had been such a crowd, she knew she hadn't seen everyone come and go. Then she noticed that one man was standing near the front window looking outside. "How can I zoom in?" She played with the mouse and found a way to enlarge the image.

She squinted at the screen and noticed that the man looked like Andrew Wright. Andrew was standing near the window, where he was approached by another man, and they seemed to have quite the conversation. He wasn't anywhere near the display case for the half hour leading up to the disappearance. In fact, he seemed relatively on the outside of the gathering.

Priscilla sat back with a frown. Carly was right. One video camera did them no good. All it did was confirm that the few people on the video at the time of the disappearance of the medal weren't anywhere near the display case.

Andrew hadn't been close, but what about Jedd, the reporter? He had known about the medal, and he wasn't near the door. Which meant he could have been by the display case.

Priscilla knew there was only one way to find out. She decided to walk down to the newspaper office and talk to Jedd, but first she needed to tell Mildred about what she'd found.

After a few minutes Mildred entered the room, her face hopeful. "Did you find something?"

"Well, I've confirmed that Andrew Wright isn't a suspect. He was in view of the camera the whole time. First staring out the window, and then talking to someone—a friend, I presume."

Mildred sat. She tapped the side of her temple. "You know, it's coming back to me. It was Jedd."

Priscilla tucked a stray strand of hair behind her ear. "What was Jedd?"

"The man Andrew was talking to." Mildred furrowed her brow as if the memory was returning. "I don't know why I didn't remember it sooner. Jedd wanted to interview Deanie, but there was a line. That's when he walked over and started asking Andrew questions. Maybe if you look at the video again..."

Priscilla rewound the video, and they watched the grainy photo of Andrew at the window. Other people walked in and out the door. After a while the man approached Andrew. His back was to the camera, and he stood mostly out of the shot, but as they watched, he pulled a small notebook and either a pen or pencil from his shirt pocket. The longer she watched, the clearer it was that Andrew was responding to the man's questions.

She'd seen enough and paused the video. "That has to be Jedd, which means I don't need to question him."

Mildred crossed her arms over her chest. "That's good news, I suppose. Two fewer suspects. At least we don't have to waste our time following those rabbit trails."

"Which means I need to get back to work. There are more places to search before we can put to rest the idea that the medal has been tucked away somewhere inside the museum."

CHAPTER EIGHTEEN

The chiming of a clock told Priscilla she had another hour before it was time to pack up and head home. The family visiting the museum had left, and the kids' frowns had turned to smiles when Priscilla told them about Candy Lane's bakery down the street. It seemed that sweets could still do the trick to turn a day around for grumpy children. Once the family stepped inside the cute shop, she was certain the day would only get better.

It had been a long day. She'd looked through the 1812 parlor, the 1850s dining room, and the 1790s pantry. There was no sign of the medal in any of those places. Priscilla placed her fingertips to her temples where the beginning of a headache was stirring.

Think. If I hid a medal somewhere in this house, where would I tuck it? She wouldn't put it someplace close to its original location. That would be too obvious and make it too easy to find. As much time as she'd spent looking, the hiding place certainly wasn't evident. She hadn't been able to confirm whether anything else had been stolen, so that didn't provide any clues either.

Priscilla paused in the doorway of the pantry and thought of that word, *confirmed.* She wondered if Lillian and Carly had filed away enough papers to provide any proof that things were indeed missing. With hurried steps she went to find Carly. Lillian was still sitting at the worktable sorting through files, but the piles were much smaller than when they'd started hours earlier. She was swaying her head and humming as she worked, and Priscilla noticed she'd put in earbuds. She could hear the faint strains of music while she watched Lillian sort and stack.

Carly, on the other hand, was on her feet and nearing the doorway to the archives as Priscilla approached.

Her wide, eager eyes focused on Priscilla. "Did you find something, Mrs. Grant? I heard your steps. They seemed excited."

"I didn't find something, but I did *think* of something." Priscilla scanned the room. "I know it's hard to confirm such things since...well, the current system makes it easy for things to be set aside and not put back where they go, but have you gone through enough documents that you can be certain that some things are missing?"

Carly nodded so hard she resembled a bobblehead toy. "We haven't gone through everything, but from what we have sorted, I can safely say the items I've been looking for are not in those piles."

Priscilla stroked her chin. "Can you show me where some of the missing things you've noticed were supposed to be?"

Carly's wide eyes grew even brighter. Her face lit up, and Priscilla could almost imagine her thoughts: *Finally, someone is listening to me.*

With short, quick steps, Carly moved to a file cabinet in the corner.

"There are very old documents in this cabinet. They were found at the house of an elderly sea captain after he passed away. He'd been collecting ancient shipping documents for a while. They were things most people throw away, but thankfully this sea captain was a hoarder. Months and years passed, and his collection grew valuable. It's incredible how even random documents become important and valuable in the light of history. Everyday things of the past give us a glimpse into how people really lived, which is simply fascinating."

"My husband Gary used to like to collect things too." Priscilla chuckled to herself. "Once an antique dealer from Omaha stopped by the farm because he heard Gary had a few old sheds filled with items. Gary made enough money off that sale to buy me a new double oven." An ache settled in her heart, but Priscilla made a conscious effort not to let her emotions get stuck there. She had work to do today. Tonight, though, she could let her mind get lost along trails of old memories.

"I know this is a lot to ask." Priscilla picked up a legal pad and pen from the table and handed them to Carly. "Can you write down as much as you remember about the documents you believe are missing? I don't expect you to get everything or even the majority, but maybe, just maybe, we can start seeing if there's a pattern to all of this." Priscilla paused before she released the pen completely. "Oh, and by the way, you can call me Priscilla."

"Sure. Good idea, uh, Priscilla. I don't know why I didn't think of that sooner." She took the pen and pad and softly tapped the pen on the side of her temple as if trying to stir up memories. "Can you give me a bit of time? Right away I can think of at least a dozen things, but it's going to take me a minute to get it all down."

"Sure, I really appreciate you doing that."

Carly sank into a wingback chair, folded her legs up crisscross on the seat, lowered her head, and began jotting notes. Mixed emotions surged through Priscilla as she watched the young woman fill a page and then another.

Priscilla was excited and worried by the list. Something deep down inside told her this was somehow tied to the missing medal. But if Carly was involved in any of the thefts, she could take them on a complete rabbit trail. Trusting her information meant trusting Carly—a person who continued to be evasive.

Yet as Priscilla studied the young woman, she didn't appear to be anything other than what she claimed: a passionate researcher who truly valued historical items and who honestly was doing all she could to call attention to their potential loss and protect the remaining items.

"Carly..." Priscilla waited until the girl looked at her. "I know you're doing all you can to help us on this search. Thank you for that. But I wonder what is it you're hiding. You don't have to tell me, but it would really help if I understood who you worked for and what you've been searching for on these trips to Martha's Vineyard."

The young woman looked up at her with furrowed brows. She studied Priscilla's face, as if trying to decide if she could be trusted. Then the concern faded, and a new vulnerability broke through as if she'd reached a decision.

With a sigh, Carly pointed to the other wingback chair. "Have a seat," she said in little more than a whisper. "This is quite a story."

Priscilla settled into the chair, crossed one ankle over the other, and leaned forward. She could hear Mildred downstairs running a vacuum. Across the room Lillian was still bopping away to the music in her earbuds. She sorted through the paperwork with concentrated effort.

Realizing there wasn't anyone who could overhear them, Carly's worried expression melted, replaced by excitement. In ten seconds' time, the mask she'd been wearing peeled from her face, shattering into a million little pieces. "Priscilla," she said in just over a whisper, "I work for a treasure hunter."

Priscilla's breath caught in her throat. That wasn't what she'd expected to hear. "A treasure hunter?"

"It sounds romantic, I know. Everyone loves hearing about sunken treasure and great riches, and that's the problem." Carly sighed, uncrossed her legs, and shifted so she was closer to Priscilla. "It's nothing like the movies."

"What do you mean?"

"Well, most treasure hunters today are just interested in wealth and status. Can you imagine all the attention someone would receive if he or she made the discovery of a lifetime? It can be absolutely life changing. The problem is they have no concern for the historical value of the wreckage. Even many archaeologists don't view historic shipwrecks as deserving the same degree of protection as archaeological sites on land. The treasure hunters plunder everything of value, and even the experts don't study these historical wrecks in depth like they should."

Carly reached over and placed a hand on Priscilla's knee. "Doesn't it seem wrong to destroy these vestiges of history? Can you imagine finding a wreck, only to have someone come and sift through everything of monetary value while not paying attention to the items of true value—the evidence of the people whose lives were forever changed by the events?"

Priscilla immediately thought of Gary. There were things outsiders might find valuable from their life together—their land, their farm equipment, their house, filled with appliances and modern conveniences. How easily someone could strip away those things "of worth" and ignore the true items of value: the faded pictures in yellowed photo albums, the crude, childish drawings of Rachel's childhood, the threadbare sweater that Gary refused to let her throw out. The memories attached to those items were worth so much more than the items themselves. They represented how she and Gary had worked together to build a meaningful and rich life.

Shipwrecks, she knew, had even more significance to eras and people. To history.

"It just doesn't seem right, you know, to destroy the last evidence of a significant period of Western history for the profit of a few people. Just think of all the generations to come who will miss the lessons."

"So what is your part? What are you doing about it?"

Carly brushed her hair back from her face, but as she released it, it returned to its place, brushing her cheek again. "Well, if you promise not to tell anyone..."

Priscilla nodded. "I promise I won't."

"Well, my employer has me looking into numerous shipwrecks in the area. Other treasure hunters already have salvage rights to the more major ones. But we're interested in ones that have been overlooked. Or if we discover that the ships are in different locations than were previously thought, we can try to get the rights ourselves—not to plunder the valuables but to protect valuable history for the good of future generations."

As Carly talked, she continued to transform before Priscilla's eyes. She was a passionate lover of history. She valued all that was held within this museum and even more beyond. No wonder she was so anxious about the security system. She'd seen or imagined history stripped away by those who thought only of themselves—their interest, their adventure, and their glory.

"It sounds like you care deeply about this, and it sounds like your employer is working on a good thing."

"It's an important thing." Carly cleared her throat. "A true archaeologist should do what they can to discourage and prevent the destruction of sites when the only purpose in doing so is to acquire materials for anything other than scientific and historic purposes."

Priscilla smiled, guessing that was a spiel that Carly had heard and was repeating—probably from her employer. "That's why I've been so frustrated. It's almost as if this museum is a shipwreck that's being looted. I guarantee that whoever is doing this is after something. Information that can help them in some way. They're acquiring materials that, first, don't belong to them, and second, are no longer available to anyone else. It's almost as if..." Carly paused and then shook her head. "Oh, never mind." She looked at the list in her hand, running her finger over the words on the page as if they held great appeal.

"Thank you for sharing everything, Carly. I promise I won't say anything, but I think that you might want to tell Mildred. In fact, why have you felt you couldn't tell her the truth?"

"Well...I didn't think she'd give me the same kind of access to the archives. I mean, it would be easy to second-guess someone like me. What if I was working for someone who wanted to loot shipwrecks instead of preserve their history? I was worried that if Mildred knew the information I was looking up centered around sunken ships and missing treasure, she'd have a hard time believing that my motives—and the motives of my employer—are pure. But besides all that, my employer and I have to be careful about who we share information with. More than once, someone has approached him, pretending to be a friend or offering to help but instead wanting vital information for the purpose of plunder. Isn't that heartbreaking?"

"Indeed. Why did you think you could trust me with the information?"

Carly looked up at Priscilla from under her long eyelashes and offered a soft smile. "Well, I've been watching you and listening...the way you've volunteered your time to help Mildred, help Deanie, and even help Lillian. You have a giving heart, and"—she chuckled—"you remind me of my mom. She just has a peaceful presence. She's a hard worker, but when trouble comes, she doesn't become frantic. You're like that. It's almost as if you know good will come out of everything in the end."

"That's nice of you to say. Your mom sounds like someone I'd like to meet some day. And my hope is that everything will turn out all right in the end. My ultimate desire is that we find the medal, but even if that doesn't happen and we simply have to order a replacement for Deanie to donate to the museum, good has come out of it. Just look at all the work you and Lillian did today helping Mildred get organized. And I have a feeling that because of your persistence Mildred might start paying more attention to security. Now..." Priscilla pointed to the list Carly held in her hand, returning her attention to the question of the missing information. "Tell me about that list."

"Well, I know some of the items are missing because I found them when I was here on my last trip, but they're no longer here. Others are documents I'm currently looking for, but can't find. I have a feeling that someone, somehow, has found out that we're interested in these particular documents and now they're looking for the same information. Except that they're stealing it so no one else can have access to it."

"But why would someone be looking for the same information? How would they know about what you're researching?"

Carly cocked an eyebrow. "If anyone connected me with my employer, it would be easy for them to find out what I was up to. My employer speaks at many conferences. He has a few friends and many enemies. Do you have any idea how many treasure hunters wish to silence him or steal his ideas?"

Priscilla chuckled. "Oh, I can only imagine." She narrowed her gaze on Carly, the pieces coming together in her mind. "So you think someone figured out who you work for and followed you, and then..."

"And then they stole everything I've been researching to stop me...stop my employer from gaining information about other wreck sites in order to loot them." Carly crossed her arms over her chest. "All we want to do is locate the sites and then protect them so we can carefully gather historically relevant items for preservation."

"So Mildred has a bigger problem than just a war medal."

"If I'm right..." Carly released a heaving sigh. "That's what I'm afraid of." She handed Priscilla the legal pad.

Priscilla scanned the list. Carly had listed various journals, newspaper stories and reports, and even a few maps—all of them missing. "I think Mildred would have a meltdown if your concerns are valid."

"That's what I'm afraid of, but I feel so helpless. History is being stolen from right under our noses, and there's nothing we can do about it."

Priscilla sighed. "If we don't find out who's been stealing from the museum, who knows how many more irreplaceable items we could lose?"

Carly nodded, and the hint of tears filled her eyes. She looked at the list again. "There seems to be too many files on my list for them all to be misplaced." She rubbed her brow. "I'm scared about who else to talk to about this because I don't know who I can trust."

"Thank you for trusting me. I promise I won't break that trust."

The vacuum from downstairs ceased, and footsteps started coming up the stairs.

Mildred entered the archive room. With a forced smile, she turned her attention to Carly. "Oh good, you're still here. I just got a phone call from someone who is interested in looking through one of our journals. She believes the author is one of her distant relatives. I'm almost sure I remember you asking about that same journal a few days ago. You can probably find it quicker than I can."

"Oh, that's interesting—" Priscilla started.

"Which journal?" Carly interrupted. She rose from the chair, took a couple of steps forward, and stood in front of Mildred, her fists clenched and her breathing heavy.

Mildred sighed, as if weary of Carly's antics. Instead of answering her directly, she turned her attention to Priscilla. "It's an old whaling journal—one of the museum's most prized possessions. It was written by the widow of one of the island's most notorious seamen."

"I know exactly which one you mean." Carly rocked back and forth on her heels. "He'd come home and tell his wife amazing stories, and she wrote them all down. We know lots of the history from the turn of the century because of that journal."

"How fascinating. I'd love to see it too. But you said that the person who requested it is related? Do you really think that's the case?" Nervous tension returned to Priscilla's gut. Was she going to doubt everyone from now on? She finally understood how Carly felt, and why her reaction to the caller's request was so strong. It was hard not to see every person who came into the museum as a possible suspect.

"Yes, that's what she said..." Even as she said those words, Mildred revealed doubt in the turn of her mouth. But then, with the set of her chin, she pushed those thoughts away. "And because that's what she said, I have no reason to doubt it."

Carly listened but didn't argue. Instead she turned her attention to a cabinet on the wall. "And, thankfully, I know just where it is." She moved to the cabinet, with Mildred and Priscilla right on her tail.

Lillian paused her humming and looked at them as if realizing for the first time that something was going on. She put the paperwork and files to the side and straightened up, as if ready to jump up and help. "Is everything all right?"

No one answered her.

Carly opened the cabinet, but as she looked through the items on the shelf, the color drained from her face. She turned to Priscilla, and tears filled her eyes. She picked up the list of missing items and added four words: *old whaling journal—missing.*

CHAPTER NINETEEN

W here is the journal?" Mildred nearly pushed Carly to the side as she moved to the cabinet.

Carly threw the tablet and pen onto the table. "It's not here."

With frantic movements Mildred started sifting through the items on the shelves. "It has to be here. It just has to be. A couple of years ago an archive in Boston asked if they could add it to their collection. But I couldn't part with it. I thought it was important that it stay here on Martha's Vineyard since it's part of our history...It was a journal, a whole journal, and not just random papers. It has to be here."

Lillian looked at Priscilla curiously, and she knew she had to fill her in on what they were discussing. "We've been looking around, and there is too much to explain but...it seems a very important and valuable journal is missing."

Lillian's hand flew to her mouth, and she made a *tsking* sound. "Oh, I'm so sorry. What a horrible thing to discover, Mildred. Are you sure you didn't move it someplace else?"

Mildred spun around, and her eyes fixed on Lillian like daggers. "No, and all of you are finding out I'm incompetent. Completely incompetent. I can't be sure about anything now, can I?"

Priscilla reached out and touched Mildred's arm. "Lillian didn't mean to suggest that. You know she didn't. And we're sorry, Mildred, that this journal is missing too."

The anger in Mildred's face melted to defeat. "Who would do this? Why would someone take that journal?" She placed a hand on her chest, took a long, deep breath, and ran a finger around her collar. "Is it getting hot in here? Oh, my chest. It's starting to ache. It literally aches to know that someone has taken this too." She sputtered as if unable to say the next few words. "Someone has really been taking our things, haven't they? They've been...robbing us."

She swayed slightly. Priscilla quickly tucked herself under one of Mildred's arms, and Carly scooted herself around and did the same under Mildred's other arm.

"I'll call the police." Lillian already had her phone out.

"Thank you. Let's head back down to the kitchen. I can get you a glass of water, Mildred. Let's go," Priscilla urged.

"I'll make you a cup of tea," Carly added.

Priscilla turned to Lillian, and her friend waved her on.

"Go on," Lillian insisted. "I can get myself down the stairs after I talk to the police. It just might take a few extra minutes to do it, but I'll be fine."

Priscilla nodded, and for the briefest moment she wondered if it was all right leaving Lillian in this room. Lillian was trustworthy, wasn't she? Priscilla believed so, but like Carly, she was starting to question everyone's motives.

"We'll see you downstairs in a minute. But please be careful coming down the stairs." Priscilla looked to the tin that had held muffins. "Would you like me to take that—carry it down for you?"

"No." The word shot from Lillian's mouth. "I'm telling you, don't worry about me." She shooed them away with a wave of her hand. "I can tuck that tin into my satchel and carry it over my arm. Please just care for Mildred."

Lillian's emphatic insistence on keeping the tin in her possession momentarily aroused Priscilla's suspicion, but she quickly admonished herself for mistrusting her friend. Lillian had shown herself to be fiercely independent and self-sufficient, and her refusal to accept help was completely in character. Feeling a bit guilty, Priscilla acknowledged that caring for Mildred was indeed her priority. She tightened her grip and with slow steps led her friend to the stairs.

"Have I really been so blind?" Mildred mumbled to herself. "I trusted people too much. Yes, that's it. I trusted they were who they said and were researching what they told me they were researching."

Mildred's arms tightened around their shoulders, depending on their support, and Priscilla looked past Mildred to Carly. If she wasn't mistaken, Carly's legs were also shaking as she took tentative steps forward.

Fear filled Carly's eyes, and for good reason. Priscilla felt sorry for the young woman. There was no doubt that if Carly tried to tell Mildred the truth of who she was and what she was researching, her confession would be met with anger and disbelief. And for the first time since their talk, Priscilla thought it best that Carly keep the truth to herself—at least for now until they could figure out their next step.

They descended the stairs and led Mildred to the kitchen and settled her into a vintage dining room chair. Carly brewed a cup of tea and brought it to her. Black, just as Mildred liked it. Mildred blew on the hot, steamy liquid and then sipped from the Styrofoam cup. It was clear from the distant look in her eyes that her thoughts were far away.

"Gone. So much gone. How could I have been so foolish?" Mildred mumbled.

They heard Lillian descending the stairs next. Priscilla focused on the *clip-clop* of the crutches then the steps of Lillian easing herself down. Finally she rounded the corner and entered the kitchen, taking a seat at the table.

The silence was deafening. Lillian looked at Priscilla with a curious gaze. "The police said they will send someone over soon."

"All right." Priscilla leaned close to Carly and said in a low voice, "While we wait for the police, it might be a good idea to share your list with Mildred. She needs to know what items you think are missing."

Carly sighed and left the table to hurry upstairs. She returned and placed the list she'd made in front of Mildred.

Mildred set her empty cup on the table. "What's this?"

"A list of other things that are missing...or at least the things we can't locate so must be missing."

Color drained from Mildred's face yet again.

Priscilla placed a hand on her friend's arm to show her support. Mildred read through the list and gasped as if she'd just been punched in the gut.

After giving Mildred a few minutes for the news to sink in, Priscilla returned to the question she'd wanted to ask for a while. "Is there a pattern? If you look at the items on this list, do you see any connections?"

Mildred placed a hand to her throat. "What do you mean?"

"I mean if we could see some type of connection, that could help us figure out who took the items or why. And then maybe we'll know if they also took the missing medal."

"I don't remember what was in every document..." Mildred turned to Carly. "But with your help..."

"I can remember most of them." Carly straightened in her seat, and the smallest bit of joy shone in her eyes. Priscilla could tell it meant a lot to the young woman that Mildred had requested her help. "I believe if we put our heads together, we can figure it out."

Priscilla's pounding heart slowed as she noticed a difference in both Mildred's and Carly's attitudes. As they scooted up to the kitchen table, with the notepad between them, it was clear they no longer saw each other as threats but as comrades.

Mildred pursed her lips as she looked at the list. "Let's start by breaking these into categories. There are journal entries, letters, newspaper reports, and records from ships' logs."

Carly flicked her hair back over her shoulder, a new light filling her face. "What's the common link?"

"Well, from the material I remember, most of these things dealt with shipping and sailing between here and Nantucket." Mildred jotted down a note, and then she paused. "I don't understand how someone could sneak so many items out. I mean, it's not like the museum is filled with visitors all the time. I'm able to keep tabs on where people are. I don't have any idea how I could have missed someone slipping into the archive room."

"Unless you were distracted. A lot was going on Tuesday night. There was even a time when guests entered the museum and we were looking outside and welcoming Deanie. I suppose someone would have had time to get up to the archive room and riffle through the files and cabinets—"

"And steal the medal while they were at it."

Priscilla snapped her fingers. "I'm having a really hard time trying to find a motive for anyone around here to steal a Congressional Gold Medal. But what if this isn't about the medal at all? What if the missing medal provided the distraction someone needed to get out of the building with the real items they wanted to take? The police were looking for a small medal, not a bag full of files and papers."

"You may be right," Mildred said. "But remember, only a handful of people knew the medal was going to be here."

Priscilla shook her head. "But any of them could have told other people about it. Or maybe someone saw the medal and took the opportunity on the spur of the moment. We may never know for sure. But I'm really beginning to think this whole situation is about these other documents that have disappeared."

"Maybe." Mildred sighed. "With everything that was happening at the party, I wasn't focused on where people were at all. Anyone could have walked out with the journal or other files right under our noses. After all, as you just said, the police were looking for a missing medal, nothing else."

The minutes continued to tick by as Carly and Mildred conferred over what they remembered about the missing items. The chiming of the clock caught Priscilla's attention again, and she startled in the seat. The museum had closed an hour ago, and they hadn't even noticed. Worse yet, Lillian was still there patiently watching them all work and not saying a word.

"Lillian, I'm so sorry." Priscilla stood. "I need to get you home. What a horrible friend I am for asking you to volunteer and then forgetting to take you home. You should have been home resting hours ago."

"Are you joking? This is the most excitement I've had in a while. Well, unless you count falling, breaking my ankle, and nearly freezing on your property. I suppose that was pretty exciting too."

Priscilla couldn't help but smile at her friend's humor, even in spite of all that had happened that day. "Just give me a minute to gather my things, and I'd be happy to give you a ride home."

"Oh, no bother. I texted Al fifteen minutes ago. He's swinging by and getting tacos to go and then picking me up.

Thankfully my husband is a very understanding and easygoing man. He has no problem with having to eat from his favorite fast-food restaurant."

Priscilla reached across the table and squeezed Lillian's hand. "You are a kind and understanding friend. I have to say that out of all the lighthouses in the world, I'm glad you fell and broke your ankle at mine." She chuckled.

"I am too." A sweet light filled Lillian's eyes.

Knowing that Lillian was taken care of, Priscilla turned her attention back to Carly and Mildred. They were talking excitedly, and Priscilla wasn't able to follow them.

"So, did you find something?" she asked.

"Yes! There is a pattern after all. Many of the missing items are from between the years 1900 and 1910." Carly nearly bounced up and down in her seat.

Priscilla nodded then froze as an idea hit her. "What about that big shipwreck? I read about it in a book by some guy named Jackson."

"Yes, I know the book that you're thinking of. It's the one about the search for the RMS *Republic*." Carly clasped her hands together. "Shawn Jackson only cares about one thing, and it's not the preservation of historical items we could salvage from the *Republic*."

"The RMS *Republic*." Priscilla tried to remember what she read. "In the book, Shawn Jackson says he has the salvage rights."

"Well, he was local." Carly huffed. "He expects finding the treasure to make him a billionaire. But there are so many theories about what may or may not have been on that ship. We don't know for sure. People have taken this fight to court and tried for more than thirty years to recover what's on the ship. It's deep enough that it isn't an easy matter to get down there and pull the items up." The young woman gestured broadly as she talked. "My employer believes that there is a wealth of historical information in that ship that should be shared."

"It's the millionaire's ship, right?" Priscilla believed that's what she'd read it was called.

"Yes, because so many millionaires used it to go back and forth across the Atlantic. But it also was the transportation for thousands of immigrants. Two thousand were on board the day it sank." Carly sighed. "Can you imagine the history we could find if we could salvage their belongings?"

"It seems a long time to hope that anything is still there and reclaimable."

"Maybe. Like I said before, Shawn Jackson is an opportunist who only cares about the gold that may or may not actually be there. He cares nothing for the history and preservation of one-of-a-kind artifacts. It hurts to think someone like that could find and profit from the treasure."

Mildred leaned back. "It's quite the story, but people have been trying to salvage that ship for many years."

"I've never heard of it." Lillian glanced at her watch. "Al should be here within five minutes, but can you give me a quick rundown?"

Priscilla explained to her about the sinking of another White Star luxury liner off the coast of Nantucket in 1909. "Unlike the *Titanic* that lost well over a thousand people, only six were killed when a cargo ship carrying immigrants struck the liner."

"I suppose after the *Titanic*, the sinking of other luxury ships paled in comparison."

"I don't know." Priscilla stroked her chin. "You'd think it wouldn't be hard to remember a ship that was carrying a secret cache of rare gold coins intended for delivery to Czar Nicholas II, worth more than a billion dollars today."

"Allegedly carrying a cache of rare gold," Mildred said. "That's a rumor, but I suppose there are those who feel the rumor is worth obtaining salvage rights for."

"Not that it stops others from searching and taking what they want." Carly huffed. "There are all types of looters in these parts."

"But isn't that illegal?" Lillian looked at them with a wide-eyed gaze. "Someone would have to be pretty gutsy to try that."

"It is illegal, but if someone is stealing from *us*, do you think they care about who has salvage rights?" Mildred's shoulders slumped again. She looked as if she were already convinced that the items taken from her museum were long gone too.

"To some people I guess it wouldn't matter what was legal and what wasn't." Lillian rose as Al pulled into the parking lot and parked. She grabbed her crutches and tucked them under her arms. "Someone who wants to find a treasure like that would give up everything else in their lives to find it. Especially when there's a billion dollars worth of gold to be found." She hobbled toward the door. "I'll wait for Al to come in. I've been wanting him to meet you ladies."

Priscilla went to the door as Al made his way up the sidewalk. "Don't hurry, Lillian. I'll let Al in." She chuckled. "It'll give me a chance to ask about his favorite taco joint. If I can't find answers tonight, maybe I can find dinner for us after we're through."

CHAPTER TWENTY

Priscilla opened the door for Al and welcomed him inside. As he stepped through the doorway wearing his work clothes and cowboy boots, a familiar ache filled her chest. A tall, lanky man with hair more gray than brown, Al looked nothing like Gary. But there was so much about the man that reminded Priscilla of her husband: the red-and-black flannel shirt flecked with bits of straw. The unbuttoned jean jacket that had been patched more than once at the elbows. And the aroma of barn and mud that made her long for Kansas, for home.

"Come on in, Al. I'm Priscilla Grant. Lillian is coming. I hope she didn't overdo it today. It's my fault really. We're caught up in some type of mystery, and we lost track of time." She gestured toward the women at the table. "We're all glad to finally meet you. This is Carly Kendricks, a student from Boston, and Mildred Pearson, who is the curator of this wonderful museum."

Al nodded. He tilted back his baseball cap and looked around the foyer, taking it all in. "It's a pleasure to meet all of you. This is a nice museum you got here. I've always wanted to come inside, but like Lillian says, my cows are my babies, and I rarely find myself away from the farm. But I'm glad Lillian could come and help all of you."

"You have a *farm* right here in Vineyard Haven?" Carly walked toward him in disbelief. "I didn't know there was such a thing. Of course, I haven't explored the island much. Usually I get right off the ferry and head here."

Al nodded and folded his arms across his chest as Lillian shuffled to his side. "Oh yes, there are a number of farms on the island. Our friends down the road have even started a dairy, and they're giving tours to visitors. 'Agritourism' they call it." He laughed. "I thought about doing that, but then I remembered how protective Lillian is of her flower garden."

"Oh yes, my garden is not for tourists. Can you imagine me trying to paint with all those people coming and going?" Lillian laughed and waved a crutch at an imaginary crowd of trespassers.

"You'd think I'd asked if I could graze my cows in her rose-bushes from the response I received when I mentioned opening our place up to kids from the city who come to the island with their parents and have never had a chance to explore a real farm. Of course, I take half the credit for her blooms. If it weren't for my soil—"

"Soil? Did you mention that you know about soil?" Mildred got up from the table and approached him. "I'm sorry, I didn't mean to interrupt, but since you're here, I have this plant." She pointed to a large fern on a stand in the corner. "It just hasn't done well in the last few months. It used to be twice as large and so green." She walked over to it and lifted one of the branches. "Look how brown the leaves are. Do you think it's the soil? It's looked especially lifeless in the last week."

"In the last week, you say?" Al gave a humored smile as he walked to join her. "Well now, I'm better with roses, but I could look it up online." He stuck his fingers into the soil and felt around. "It does feel a little dry, and I can tell it's root-bound, which could be another problem. A larger pot might work. Or..." Al stopped talking, and he got a curious look on his face. He put both hands into the pot and started to dig. With a wondering look he pulled something out and held it up to the light. Then he grinned. "Or maybe there's something in this Congressional Gold Medal that the plant doesn't like."

A loud squeal erupted in the room, and it took a second for Priscilla to realize that it was coming from her. Carly called out with delight, and Mildred moved to the chair behind the front counter and plopped herself into the seat.

"I can't believe it," she murmured. "It really *has* been here all the time. I just can't believe it." She gave a subdued laugh. "I knew I needed to water that thing."

Carly started bouncing up and down and clapped her hands together. "Then what Priscilla said was right. The theft of the medal—it was a distraction all along."

"Well, I suppose someone could have buried it and planned on coming back later." Lillian stood at the door on her crutches and for the first time she looked weary. "Maybe that's something we can figure out another day."

Priscilla strode up to Al, and he offered the medal to her. It was larger and heavier than she had imagined it would be. She brushed the dirt from the surface and looked into the face of the WASP pilot who was staring off into the distance with an optimistic hope for the future. Even though Deanie wasn't the model for the medal, Priscilla could imagine a young Deanie having the same hopeful expectation in her eyes.

Priscilla smiled at the image. "I can't wait to tell Deanie what we found."

There was a knock on the door, and Officer April Brown stood there, her shoulder-length hair in a ponytail. "We got a call that you needed to report a theft."

Mildred nodded. "There may be more than one."

Lillian and Al excused themselves. "We have tacos waiting in the car, and my ankle is throbbing. Will you call me tomorrow, Priscilla, and let me know how everything goes with Deanie?"

"Of course, and thank you for all your help today." Priscilla gave Lillian hug. "I'll be sure to call you and update you about Deanie and…well, everything else that's happening around here."

"Do you need to talk to us, Officer?" Al gave her his attention.

"I'm not sure. Someone needs to fill me in on what's happened before I'll know." She looked at Mildred and then Lillian. "Which one of you called it in?"

"I did." Lillian's cheeks colored. "I really don't know what's going on, though."

Mildred nodded. "Unfortunately, she doesn't know anything." She sighed and scrubbed her hands over her eyes. "That didn't come out the way I meant. Lillian called you, but Carly and I are the ones who know what's missing."

Officer Brown looked at Al and Lillian. "You two don't have to stay. I'll stop by the house if I need anything, all right?"

"Sure, that will be fine." Lillian pointed at her foot. "This is keeping me pretty close to home most of the time."

Priscilla watched them go, the medal resting heavy in her hands. Then she turned to Officer Brown. "We also have the recovery of a lost item to report."

"You found the medal." Officer Brown's smile lit up her face.

"Yes, it was here all along. We just found it buried in the soil in that plant." Priscilla brushed more dirt from its surface. "I can't wait to return it to Deanie."

"Let me take down some information, and then we can let you go tell her the good news." Officer Brown turned to Mildred and Carly. "Tell me what's brought me out here."

It took the women fifteen minutes of occasionally talking over each other to explain all that had happened. Mildred wiped tears from her cheek. "I don't know how to explain it other than to say vital historical documents owned by the museum are gone."

Officer Brown jotted another couple of lines in her notebook. "Understood." She pointed at the list. "And this is your best guess of what's missing?"

"Yes." Mildred nodded, looking miserable.

"We may add items to it, but I think it's an accurate start." Carly glanced at Mildred as if she hated to mention more could be missing.

Priscilla guessed only time would tell exactly what had disappeared or been taken. But maybe Mildred would discover ways to better organize the archives and gain the security that was needed to keep a similar event from occurring in the future. Then good would come from this stressful and disheartening situation.

"Do you have any ideas who took these items?" Officer Brown focused on Mildred.

Mildred's face crumpled, and it looked like she was ready to cry. "Unfortunately, no. Maybe I've been too lax with some of the operating procedures."

Carly rolled her eyes, but Priscilla was proud of her for not saying anything to add to Mildred's guilt. "There's one person you might want to check into," Carly said.

Officer Brown raised an eyebrow. "Who?"

"Many of the missing items are related to shipping lanes and information pertaining to a narrow period of time."

"Okay?"

Carly took a breath and then plunged ahead. "I think it's all tied to the search for a ship that sank around the same time the *Republic* did. The *Liverpool* could have immense value as well. I've been thinking about this. We've known where the *Republic* is for thirty years. There's no reason to steal material that documents its whereabouts. What if the person who stole the items from the archives is looking for information regarding the sinking of the *Liverpool*?"

Mildred shrugged as if it didn't matter. "It's possible, but it doesn't change the fact that the items are missing."

"But it might help us identify who took them." Priscilla watched Carly. What did she know that she still hadn't told them?

"What makes you think this is about finding a sunken ship?" Officer Brown poised her pen over the notepad. "Are you a treasure hunter?"

Carly shook her head vehemently. "No. I'm a historian and archaeologist."

"And that brought you to our island?"

"Yes." Carly pressed her lips together as if she wouldn't say another word.

Priscilla wondered how much treasure could actually be recovered from any of these sites. "You must really believe there's billions to be made from these ships."

"It doesn't matter what I think," Carly protested. "All that matters is that my boss and his competitor are locked in a head-to-head battle to reach the same locations. The man with the current salvage rights for the RMS *Republic* could lose them at any time, and we all want to be ready to move as soon as he does. But it clearly isn't my boss behind the thefts, since the items went missing when I wasn't even on the island."

"But they were here when you came to do your preliminary search." Priscilla watched her carefully. Could Carly have taken the valuable artifacts during her first trip to Martha's Vineyard?

"Yes. They were absolutely here, and they were here when I left, or I wouldn't have returned." Carly crossed her arms over her chest.

"I need some names." Officer Brown watched Carly closely. "Who is this boss you're talking about? And who are his competitors?"

"Fine." Carly spit out the word. "My boss is Alexander Rathbone. The person who is trying to beat him to the salvage rights is Collins Allister. He's battled with the rights owner for years. Stealing artifacts would be just the kind of thing he would do to get around the law and do what he wants."

"Can you come with me to the station and give me more information?"

"Sure. As long as this helps us find the documents."

"Thank you." Officer Brown pocketed her notebook and turned to Mildred. "I'll keep you posted. If you think of anything helpful, be sure to let us know."

"Absolutely." Mildred's face was pale as Officer Brown headed to the front door, Carly on her heels. "Well, that is not how I expected the day to proceed."

Priscilla put an arm around her friend. "I know. My head is absolutely spinning. I wonder if this Collins Allister has something to do with the missing documents." And why wouldn't Carly have just told them the names of her boss and his competition earlier? Then again, if millions were at stake, secrecy was probably of utmost importance.

"I must rethink how we operate here." Mildred put a hand to her forehead. "I don't want to think about what else could have walked out that I don't even know to look for."

"You'll be able to do this. I know you will."

The front door opened, and Carly reentered. "I was able to answer the officer's questions without having to go to the station. So what's next?"

Priscilla looked down at the medal she was still holding. She shook her head. "I really can't believe it's been here the whole time." She laughed, joy bubbling through her. "We searched, we questioned, and we pondered, and it was buried in that plant the whole time."

"Yes, that solves one of the problems." Carly approached and looked more closely at the medal as Priscilla held it toward her. "But as far as I'm concerned, we've solved only the smallest part of the whole mystery. I really think, considering all the items that are missing, that someone is searching for the RMS *Liverpool*."

Mildred rubbed her temples. "That's a problem for another day. We should take a moment and celebrate the fact that the medal is found, especially knowing how much it means to Deanie."

Mildred approached Priscilla and held out her hand. Priscilla placed the medal in Mildred's palm. Mildred blew out a sigh of relief—the breath Priscilla knew she'd been holding for the week since the medal had disappeared.

"We're all exhausted," Mildred said. "I can't think of anything better than a bowl of soup for dinner, a hot bath, and bed. I'll tell you what. Priscilla, why don't you get some rest tonight and then take this medal to Deanie in the morning?"

"Me?" Priscilla placed a hand over her heart. "You trust this in my hands?"

"Of course." Mildred smiled. "You've worked so hard to find it. I know it's as safe in your hands as anywhere."

Carly stepped forward, eagerness bright on her face. "What about me? Can I go with you in the morning, Priscilla? I would love to see Deanie's face when you show her the medal."

"Actually…" Mildred turned to Carly. "I was hoping to get your help tomorrow. I'm going to have to make sure we reported all the stolen items we can to the police. I want to look more carefully and thoroughly through our archives. Can you come back and help me with a more formal list? Maybe we can discuss ways to improve processes and security while we search."

Carly offered a shy smile. "Yes, I'd love to help you, Mildred. Thank you for asking me. When I get home, I'll go over our notes again to see if I remember anything else we missed."

Priscilla and Mildred looked at each other. Priscilla could feel weariness pressing her down and thought she saw the same reflected on Mildred's face. Yet when she looked at Carly, the young woman acted as awake and perky as she had when she'd arrived this morning.

"Energy and stamina are wasted on the young." Mildred sighed.

Priscilla nodded. "Yes, and I think Deanie would say the same. Thank you for trusting me with the medal, Mildred. And for giving me the chance to brighten a war hero's day."

CHAPTER TWENTY-ONE

The next morning Priscilla woke before her alarm or Jake. She could feel the pulsing excitement at the thought of seeing Deanie and watching the dear woman's face when she placed the Congressional Gold Medal in her hands. The medal would be back home with the woman who had earned it so many years ago through her service during World War II.

As soon as Priscilla's feet hit the floor, Jake stood and stretched each leg before doing his own version of downward dog. Then he bounded toward her with a happy grin. Priscilla laughed as she rubbed behind his ears. "Let me get dressed, boy. Then we'll go for a quick walk."

The early morning routine went smoothly, with Priscilla inhaling the crisp sea air while Jake tugged at the leash and nosed the foam along the beach. Then a quick breakfast of scrambled eggs and toast followed by sweet time with the Lord as she read a psalm and then prayed. The rhythm of the morning felt right and pure. It was a morning she wanted to bottle for those moments when her gaze slid to the empty chair at the table. She needed to remind herself that it might be empty, but it didn't mean God had left her. Instead, He filled the empty places with Himself and His gifts.

She found a blank page in her journal and filled it with a fresh list of reasons she was thankful. It might be an activity fit for November, but this was a practice she should adopt all year long. A way to return her heart and mind to all she had to be grateful for. There were so many things. Not the least of which was that this morning she would be able to return the medal to Deanie. Oh, she could not wait to do that and see the delight on Deanie's face.

After she finished getting ready for the day, Priscilla made a batch of scones and packaged four to take with her to Deanie. It would be a slightly sweet treat for her new friend, something they could enjoy with a cup of tea or mug of coffee.

The drive to the nursing home was delightful, the tree branches stark against the blue sky without the leaves to cover them. The earth was settling down for the winter, and Priscilla snuggled deeper into her coat. What would her first winter on the island be like? She was about to experience it, ready or not.

When she arrived at the home, the lady at the front desk directed Priscilla to the morning room. When she entered it, she found several tables with people clustered around them. At one table a couple of elderly women worked a detailed puzzle, while at another table a rousing game of train dominoes was being played by some men. At another table, Priscilla spotted Deanie. She had an afghan across her lap and an open Bible in front of her. As she got closer, Priscilla noted that many of the verses were marked and the pages appeared to be separating from the spine.

"That's a well-loved book." Priscilla smiled as Deanie looked up at her.

"So it is, so it is." Deanie smiled at Priscilla. "What brings you here today?"

"Good news."

"Oh." Deanie's eyes sparkled. "I love good news."

Priscilla laughed with delight. "And I love delivering it." She gestured to the chair next to Deanie's. "Do you mind if I join you for a bit?"

"Of course not. Please do." She clasped her hands on top of the Bible and waited for Priscilla to sit. "All right. I've waited long enough. Tell me this good news."

"We found your medal."

Deanie's hands moved to her chest, and her eyes filled with tears. "Oh, that's wonderful."

"You'll never believe where we found it. After all the people we talked to and places we looked, someone had tucked it into the dirt in one of the plants at the museum." Priscilla pulled a cloth pouch from her bag and handed it to Deanie. "I cleaned it last night, so you can't even tell."

Deanie took the bag with trembling fingers. "I don't know how to thank you."

"There's no need. I'm not the only one who was looking for it, and I'm not even the one who found it." Warmth filled her as she watched the woman eagerly fumble with the fabric pocket before pulling the gold medallion free.

"Oh my." Deanie clutched the medal to her chest. "I never really thought we'd get this back. You said you weren't the only one looking for it?"

"That's right. Mildred at the museum also searched for it this week."

"Well, I am very grateful that you both kept looking after everyone said the medal was gone."

"I do have one request."

"Yes?"

"Could you please not tell anyone that it's been found yet?"

"Andrew will need to know."

"As long as he understands that we need to keep the information to ourselves for a bit longer. We're in the middle of looking for other items and don't want whoever took those to know we've found the medal."

Confusion clouded Deanie's eyes. "But why?"

"We think this person used your party to steal other items from the museum."

"Oh my." Deanie clutched the medal closer. "But how would they have done that?"

"We're not sure yet. The museum was so full that night with everyone there to celebrate you that it would have been easy to slip upstairs to the archives."

"You mean someone took things from there? Oh dear, that's terrible."

"It is, but now that Mildred knows the items are missing, the police have been alerted. If your medal hadn't been stolen, it might have taken a long time for someone to notice that the other items were missing too." Because without the theft of Deanie's medal, Mildred might have continued to ignore Carly. Now the two women could work together to preserve the history collected in the archives. If they were able to do that, then the losses would bring a positive outcome. "So if you'll wait a few days to let anyone know other than Andrew, that would be a big help."

"I certainly want to give you the best opportunity to find the thief."

"Thank you. Maybe if he doesn't realize we know what he's done, he'll try again after a few more security cameras and other policies are installed."

"I don't know if I should be bothered or grateful that my medal was the distraction." Deanie held the medal close to her heart. "However, I am grateful that you found the medal. Where did you find it again?"

"Buried in a potted plant. Al Salisbury was looking at the soil for Mildred and found it. He had come to pick up Lillian from the museum."

"Such a nice couple."

"You know them?"

"Of course. The island is a small place. When you've lived here as long as I have, you know most people."

"I've just met them, but already I like Lillian very much."

"I can see why you would." Deanie reached forward and clasped Priscilla's hand. "Lillian is a dear but has always been a bit of a solitary soul. Her artistic talents lend themselves to isolation, and she's been content with that."

"I met her when she came to paint the lighthouse."

"Delightful."

"Yes, except she broke her ankle while she was painting. I took her to the hospital, and we've been helping each other since."

"One can never have too many friends." Deanie said the words with a beautiful light in her eyes. "Have I ever told you about my flying friends?"

"Just a bit." Priscilla leaned forward. "I'd love to hear more."

For the next hour or so, Deanie regaled Priscilla with stories about her WASP friends and the trials they endured as they flew planes to free the men to go overseas. "Not everyone was grateful for our help. We displaced men who wanted to stay stateside. But we persevered and prevailed."

"What you did is so inspiring."

"We just did the job that was in front of us."

"No. If that was all you were doing, you could have taken a job that didn't threaten your life." Priscilla smiled at her friend then glanced at her watch. She was startled to see that almost two hours had passed since she'd arrived at Vineyard Village. "I can't believe I've taken so much of your time."

"Time is something I have in abundance right now." Deanie held up the medal and kissed it. "Thank you again for all you did to find this."

"It was an honor. Now please remember that we need you to keep quiet for at least a few days about its recovery."

Deanie made a motion like she was locking her lips. "Mum's the word. We got lots of practice at keeping secrets in the war."

"I'm sure you did." Priscilla tried to smile, but as she glanced around the room, she realized it was possible that the cat was already out of the bag. She prayed the other residents and their visitors had been so focused on what they were doing that they'd ignored Deanie and her medal. "We really need the time to find whoever is behind the thefts."

"What were they stealing again?"

"Things related to shipping routes."

"That's not very interesting." Deanie frowned.

"It can be when it might be related to a shipwreck that is rumored to have a large treasure onboard."

"The RMS *Republic*." Deanie chuckled as Priscilla felt her jaw drop. "Don't look so surprised. I've lived a long time and heard many stories. That's the only shipwreck around here that's been the focus of treasure hunters." She snorted. "I'm not convinced they'll ever find anything worth keeping. Do you know how far down that wreck is? Almost six hundred feet. That's too far for humans to go without significant assistance."

"But still, the possibility of finding hidden treasure might tempt someone to steal from the archives. Greed is a major motivator." Priscilla didn't see any need to divert Deanie's attention from the *Republic* to the *Liverpool*.

"Has been from the beginning of time." Deanie tapped a finger on the medal she'd set on her lap. "One of my friends here at Vineyard Village is Shawn Jackson's father."

His name was familiar, but Priscilla couldn't place why.

"He's the man with the salvage rights to the *Republic*. According to my friend, his son is just one good-luck opportunity away from success." She shrugged. "I'll believe it when I see it. We've been hearing predictions like that since the early 1980s when the shipwreck's location was identified."

"Do you think I could meet Shawn's father?" Priscilla felt her heart beat faster. Could this be the break they were looking for? Was it possible that Vineyard Village held the answers to their questions?

"Shouldn't be a problem." Deanie glanced at the wall clock with its big, bold numbers. "This time of day Elmer's headed to the cafeteria for an early lunch. He says he likes to beat the crowd. I think he just wants the first pick of dessert."

"Sounds like my kind of man."

"Can you help me up?" Deanie held out her arm, and Priscilla stood and helped her ease to her feet. Deanie slid the medal back into the fabric pouch then tucked it into the small bag she'd already slid her Bible into.

"Do you need a wheelchair?" Priscilla glanced around the room and noticed a couple against the wall near the door.

"I mainly use one when I'm outside the buildings. Around here they've placed chairs every so often so us old people can rest when we need to. There's also a nice handrail along the walls. Makes it easy for me if you don't mind taking it slow."

"Not at all." Soon they were toddling down the hallway and into another large room that was filled with circular tables. A buffet lined the far side, and a few people were already staking out spots at the tables.

Deanie walked straight to one gentleman. "Elmer Jackson," she said loudly. "I'd like you to meet my friend Priscilla."

The man turned to them and twisted a knob on his hearing aid as he did. Sparkling blue eyes met Priscilla's. "No need to yell, Deanie." He pointed to her. "This woman is convinced I'm deaf. I really think she's the one who needs help. All those years flying will do some serious damage to your ears."

"Aren't you one to talk?" Deanie swatted his shoulder in a way that showed how friendly their relationship was. "Priscilla wondered if she could ask you a few questions."

The man straightened his sloped shoulders and swiped the few strands of white hair he had left into formation. "Glad to help if I can, though I'm not sure what you'd want to know from an old codger like me."

Deanie plopped into the seat next to him then tried to tug out the chair on her other side. "Have a seat, Priscilla. Once you wind Elmer up, it can be a challenge to get him to slow down long enough to breathe."

"Now that's not a nice way to talk to someone you want a favor from." Elmer eyed Deanie then winked at Priscilla. "Ask away. I'm glad to help if I can."

Priscilla smiled as she looked at the table. There was a notepad in front of Elmer with the words *Bowen* and *hotel* written on it followed by a phone number and couple of other words. She focused on how she should approach him, then decided that just asking her question was probably best. "What can you tell me about your son's interest in the RMS *Republic*?"

CHAPTER TWENTY-TWO

Elmer blinked a moment then swiped his hair again. "Well, I wasn't expecting that question."

"We ladies like to keep you guessing." Deanie pursed her lips then kept going. "I already told Priscilla that Shawn has the salvage rights to the ship. Lot of good it will do him."

"That's what I keep telling him. But you know as well as I do that you can't tell these kids anything. They think they know it all."

"Don't they though."

Priscilla listened to the two with amusement. "Really, I'm just curious why he's involved with the *Republic*."

"He grew up on the island. Was just a teen when the wreck was found. There was such romance to the idea of all that gold resting on the bottom of the ocean."

"So he decided to go after it then?"

Elmer shrugged his thin shoulders. "Maybe. All I know is he started talking about it and hanging around the recovery efforts. Then he went to college but dropped out to become a deep-sea diving instructor."

"Really?" Priscilla hadn't gotten the feeling that Shawn had any professional qualifications for the recovery efforts from listening to

Carly. But maybe that was the rivalry playing out in front of her. "What did he do as a deep-sea diver?"

"Got certified and worked on some digs over the summers. Something I never quite understood in the English Channel as well as the Mediterranean. He really likes looking for old things the rest of us consider junk." He shook his head. "I've never understood it. Just had to accept that was what he liked. I never expected him to pull his brother into the hunt. Bowen was always the practical one."

Priscilla frowned at the name she'd seen on his notepad. "Bowen?"

"Bowen Thorton. My wife left me and remarried. Had Bowen a few years later. He's a good eight years younger than Shawn but successful in the best sense of the word."

"So he's interested in the wreck too?"

"I didn't think he ever would be, but lately he's been hanging around the island and all the two of them talk about is recovering sunken treasure." Elmer snorted. "It's such a fool's errand. They've gone from talking day and night about the *Republic* to some other shipwreck that happened around here. It ain't natural to go digging around for something that's rested at the bottom of the ocean for a good hundred years."

"I wonder why they're working together."

Deanie chuckled lightly as she studied Elmer. "Those two are just scheming together. The way I understand it, it's about time they saw eye to eye on something."

"It's strange though," Elmer muttered. "Bowen is an aquatic archaeologist, and he and Shawn used to fight all the time about what Shawn wanted to do with the *Republic*. Bowen used to advocate that sunken ships should be protected and preserved for future generations, but lately they talk like they're a team." He shook his head. "I'll never understand those two."

As Priscilla listened to Deanie and Elmer go back and forth about the boys and what they were up to, her heart began to pound. Elmer said that the two men were discussing another shipwreck these days. If Shawn had been chasing the *Republic* for years without success, then it made sense that he might have transferred his interest to the *Liverpool*, like Carly said. And if Bowen had suddenly decided to throw in his lot with Shawn, it was even more likely that with his training, he would understand the significance of the journals and maps in a way that Shawn might not.

It all came back to a sunken ship and the efforts to recover rumored treasure. "How are they financing the search?" Priscilla asked. Deanie and Elmer looked at her as though she'd lost her marbles and interrupted an important dialogue. "I'm sorry, but my understanding is that treasure hunting at such a depth is terribly dangerous and expensive."

Elmer nodded. "That's why the other guy had to finally give up. It took thirty years, but he ran out of pockets to chase. Shawn decided he could try next. Not sure how. He barely has two nickels to rub together most days." He shrugged as his fingers tapped the tabletop. "He's definitely not getting it from me."

Deanie patted his hand. "It's all right, Elmer. You don't need to fund the boy's delusions."

Priscilla chuckled at the idea that a middle-aged man was a boy. "Deanie, I thought of one more question. Did you see either of Elmer's boys at your birthday party?"

"Oh, I wouldn't know. I don't believe so, but there were so many people there. I'm sure I missed some of them."

"Sure. We all did." Priscilla smiled as she cataloged all that she'd learned. "Well, I need to get going. Thank you both for your time."

"Can you wait just a minute?" Deanie struggled to stand, and Priscilla eased a hand under her arm to assist her. "I just remembered something I need to tell you on the walk to my room."

"All right. It was nice to meet you, Mr. Jackson."

"You come back anytime you like. It's nice to see a young thing like you around here." He waggled his eyebrows at her in a way that set her to laughing.

"I'll be sure to do that, sir." She kept a slow pace as she and Deanie headed toward the door. "Are you sure you don't want to stay and eat your lunch?"

Deanie shook her head. "It's more important to fill you in." She looked both ways as if making sure no one could overhear. "I forgot to tell you that since it looked like my medal was gone, Andrew did the sweetest thing."

"Oh?"

"Yes, he helped me call and order a replacement medal. I didn't know something like that was even possible."

Priscilla led Deanie to a chair sitting against the hallway wall. "That was very thoughtful of him."

"Yes, it was. He does things like that. Seems to know what I want even when I won't voice it." Deanie sank against the seat with a quiet sigh. "That does feel good."

"Now you'll have two."

"Well, I had a thought. Through all of this I realized how much Andrew really does want my Congressional Gold Medal. I guess I always thought he was just humoring me." She shook her head. "I'm at the age where people think I'm wise, but sometimes I'm just an old fool. He really does think the medal is an important piece of our family history. And here I gave it away without a thought for his desires."

"Well, it is yours."

"I know, but I've decided I'd like to ask Mildred if she'd be willing to have the copy of the medal when it arrives. Then I can give Andrew the real one." Deanie turned her gaze on Priscilla. "Do you think she'd consider it?"

"I'm sure she'd think about it. Giving the replacement is generous when you don't have to give her anything."

"I don't want to be selfish, but I hadn't realized how much it means to him."

Priscilla crouched in front of Deanie. "Deanie, you have to do what you think is best. Giving the original to Andrew now that we've found it sounds like a perfect idea. I can tell Mildred for you."

"That would be nice." Deanie patted Priscilla's shoulder. "Thank you."

"My pleasure. Now, before I leave, just remember that you can't tell anyone about the medal being found. I'll be sure to let you know when that wonderful news is shareable."

Deanie's gaze followed an orderly pushing a wheelchair toward the cafeteria door. "I won't tell anyone."

"You can't tell anyone about Shawn Jackson or Bowen either."

"Or the way the brothers might be stealing things from the museum?"

Priscilla bit down a smile. "Exactly." She straightened. "Can I help you get anywhere before I leave?"

"No, I'll just slip the medal into my room and then come back for a bite to eat." Deanie struggled to her feet. "Thank you again for finding my treasure for me. I know you worked hard to do that."

Priscilla watched Deanie as she made her way down the hallway. The woman stopped several times to exchange a word with someone. The people she spoke with seemed to blossom from even a brief greeting. It was beautiful to watch her share life with others as she had with Priscilla. Then Priscilla turned and headed to the door.

As she reached the door, she froze. Jedd Patterson was pushing through the doors. "Hello, Jedd." She forced a smile that she didn't feel. "What brings you here?"

"Scouting out my next story." His smile was excited. "Did you know that since I broke the story about what happened with Deanie's medal, I've been asked to report for the local radio station?"

"No. That's great." She tried to find any sort of agenda lurking on his face. "Why come here?"

"I'm here to visit a relative."

"That's great." But Priscilla still felt a nudge of concern. "Who is it?"

"A great-aunt. Not someone you would know."

"I'm sure you're right. I'm too new to the island to know many people." Priscilla stepped back through the door. "I think many of the residents are headed to lunch."

"That's one reason I came now." His grin was boyish, and he rubbed his hands together as if anticipating something. "I'm not much of a cook, so I plan my visits for meal times. My aunt likes the company, and I enjoy eating something that isn't a microwave dinner."

Priscilla glanced over her shoulder and noted that Deanie wasn't in the hall anymore. She hoped that meant her friend was in her room and would stay there until Jedd was gone. She wasn't sure why, but she felt unsettled at the thought that Jedd was in the building moments after she'd said goodbye to Deanie. It would be so easy for him to swing by Deanie at a lunch table and ask how she was doing. Then without thought, Deanie could let it slip that the medal had been found. A carefully worded question, and Deanie could then tell him that there might be treasure hunters who may have stolen items from the museum.

"I just remembered something I need to do before I leave." Priscilla hiked her purse up her shoulder. "It was good to see you again, Jedd. Congratulations on your success."

"Thanks."

She could feel his gaze on her as she slipped away from the front doors and down the hallway Deanie had walked down. After she turned a corner, she found Deanie's room. The door was cracked, so she rapped gently on the door. "Deanie? It's Priscilla. I had one more question for you."

There was no answer, but Priscilla eased the door open, certain her friend wouldn't have left it open if she weren't in her room. What she saw brought a genuine smile to her lips. Deanie must have used up all her energy working her way down the hallway and talking with her friends, for she sat in her recliner, feet elevated and mouth open as she snoozed.

She stepped back into the hallway and eased the door shut, this time all the way.

There was no need to warn Deanie about Jedd if the old woman was asleep.

Surely he wouldn't enter a sleeping woman's room. And why would he? She was over thinking things and making it more sinister than anything the man intended. He was simply visiting a relative, and she had more important things to do like follow up on what she'd learned about Elmer's son and his half brother.

To do that, she needed to consult Mildred.

CHAPTER TWENTY-THREE

Instead of heading home, Priscilla drove to the East Shore Historical Museum. A group of Boy Scouts were bundled up and raking the last of the leaves from the museum's yard. It wouldn't be long and snow would replace the leaves as a blanket for the lawn. Several cars were parked in the lot, and Priscilla knew she'd have to wait to share her news with Mildred. If the visitors needed her assistance, Mildred would give them her full attention for as long as necessary. It was part of her charm and what made the museum so attractive.

When she entered the foyer, several matronly women were clustered around Mildred at the reception desk. Mildred pointed at a brochure she'd splayed across the desk. "So those are our exhibits. If you have any questions, don't hesitate to ask."

The women murmured their thanks then separated into pairs and wandered into different rooms.

Mildred glanced up at her, expectation lighting her face. "How is Deanie doing?"

"She was absolutely delighted when I gave her the medal." Priscilla stepped closer and lowered her voice. "You won't believe this, but I learned more about Shawn Jackson and what he's up to these days while I was there."

"Oh?" Mildred's eyebrows peaked. "We should get Carly before you say more." She glanced at the women who were engrossed in the rooms. "In fact, we can go upstairs for a few minutes and you can fill us in."

Priscilla followed Mildred up the stairs. "Have you gotten a lot done?"

"We've developed a plan, so that's encouraging." Mildred paused and turned back to Priscilla. "Carly was right all along. I had let things get too lax but was too prideful to address the problem. With her help, we'll create policies that will work for me while preserving the items entrusted to the museum."

"That's great." Priscilla was thrilled to see some good coming from the thefts. When they entered the archives, Carly was seated at the long table with several legal pads of paper spread in front of her. She looked up as they entered the room.

"Is everything okay?"

Priscilla nodded. "Yes. Deanie was thrilled to get her medal back, but we're up here because Deanie introduced me to Shawn Jackson's father, who verified that Shawn is researching local shipwrecks."

Carly's eyes widened, and her mouth dropped open. It took her a few seconds to respond. "Really? I knew it!"

"Let's not get too excited just yet." Priscilla pulled out a chair and sat. "What you don't know is that Shawn's half-brother, Bowen, is working with him now."

"Bowen?" Carly frowned and picked up her pencil and started tapping it against the paper. "Wait. He's a well-respected archaeologist. What would he be doing working with a treasure hunter like Shawn?"

"Who knows why people forsake their principles? All I know is that the brothers have gone from interest in the *Republic* to interest in another local shipwreck. My guess is that you're right, Carly, and they're researching the *Liverpool's* shipping routes and weather maps."

"If you're right, then they could very well be the ones stealing the documents." Mildred's frown suggested caution.

"Oh, she's right." Carly pushed back and stood. "This is quite a shock, finding out that Bowen is working with Shawn." She started pacing. "Bowen used to work with my boss, and I think they're still in contact. I can text Mr. Rathbone to find out."

Priscilla nodded. "That would be helpful. Does Bowen have any connection to Collins Allister?"

"I have no idea. I don't understand why Bowen would work against Mr. Rathbone's interests. I've always understood they were friends as well as colleagues." Carly pulled her phone from her bag and started texting. "I had no idea he was in town, which makes me sure Mr. Rathbone doesn't know either."

"Do you know him? Bowen, I mean?"

"No. I wouldn't be able to pick him out of a lineup. I've only heard my boss talk about him or to him on the phone." Carly looked up from her texting. "You have to understand. I haven't worked for Mr. Rathbone for long. This is a trial run that I hope will lead to a permanent position."

"Well, I know Shawn, and I want to go talk to him about Bowen and what they're up to." Mildred turned to Carly. "Would you be willing to stay downstairs and help anyone who comes in while we're gone?"

"Yes! Absolutely." Carly smiled as she scooped up her materials from the table. "I'll use the time to come up with ideas for more security downstairs."

"Don't get too carried away, but I'll be grateful for your help."

Priscilla couldn't believe the change the last day had brought in the relationship between the two women. It was heartwarming to watch Mildred welcome the young woman rather than merely tolerate her.

"I don't want to take time to change." Mildred gestured at her late 1700s costume. "Let's get moving."

"I can drive as long as you can direct me."

"No problem."

The drive to Shawn's house was quiet, only the hushed voices of talk radio filling the space with noise.

Mildred leaned forward and turned up the volume. "I didn't just hear that, did I?"

"Hear what?" Priscilla focused on the interview.

"We are interrupting our replay of last night's weekly highlights for an interview with local celebrity Deanie Spangler."

"What on earth?" Priscilla felt dread rise in her at the thought of what Deanie would say. "I cautioned her not to talk to anyone."

"Well, she's talking." Mildred crossed her arms over her chest. "We should have kept the medal until we were done with the investigation."

"Maybe, but it was a relief to give it to her today and know she had it." Priscilla turned up the volume.

"Jedd Patterson is here with an interview he conducted this morning."

"He didn't let any moss grow under his feet." Priscilla sighed as she slowed for a Stop sign. "I didn't think he'd wake a sleeping woman."

"She was sleeping?" Mildred's voice became shrill. "Then she'll spill everything."

"This morning I had the opportunity to speak with local legend Deanie Spangler." Jedd's voice was smooth as honey, as if he had been created to work in radio. "She was a delight as always, and it was great to find her in good spirits after last week's terrible theft. Here's a part of our interview:

"Ms. Spangler, it's so good to see you again."

"You too, Jedd." Deanie's voice was alert and spry.

"Have you recovered from the loss of your medal?"

"Definitely. My friend returned the medal to me this morning. I was so thrilled."

"That is wonderful. Do you know who stole it?"

"Well, it turns out whoever took it just hid it in the museum. In a plant, of all things. Can you believe that?"

"That's incredible." He paused, and Priscilla held her breath. So far nothing devastating had been shared. "Do they know who took it?"

"Oh no." Her voice softened as if she were leaning forward to whisper. "But the theory is it has something to do with the RMS *Republic*."

"Really? That's fascinating."

"It is. Seems people will never get tired of searching for that treasure. If only they cared as much for chasing after the things that really matter—like God and friendship."

"Yes, well, why would they hide it in the museum?"

"To create a distraction. Can you believe somebody wanted some old papers from there?" Deanie's voice got softer again. "But I'm not really supposed to tell anyone, so let's keep this between you and me."

As she listened to the announcer wrap up the interview, Priscilla fumed. "I cannot believe Jedd would take advantage of a one-hundred-year-old woman."

"Some people like publicity."

"Not Deanie. I'm certain that Jedd never mentioned this would be a radio interview. Deanie knew how important it was to keep this information private."

"Well, I hope Shawn and Bowen didn't hear the interview. Although, Deanie didn't mention the *Liverpool*, so that's at least something in our favor." Mildred pointed to a cross street. "Turn there. Shawn's house is just down that road."

A minute later Priscilla pulled into a driveway. Mildred climbed from the car but frowned as she scanned the house. "Those tricycles don't belong here. Shawn doesn't have any children."

"Let's knock on the door and see who's here."

They climbed the steps to the front door. The cottage was charming, with a fresh coat of white paint with red details. Plastic covered the windows in preparation for the winter cold. When they knocked on the door, a young woman answered it, a toddler and young boy peeking around her. "Hello?"

"Hello. I'm Mildred, and this is my friend Priscilla. We're looking for Shawn Jackson."

"I'm sorry, but he doesn't live here. We bought the house from him a year ago."

"Do you have any idea where he's moved?"

"I think he bought a farm on the edge of the island."

"Thank you. Sorry to bother you." Priscilla turned and headed to the car, Mildred right behind her. "Let's see if we can find information on him, and then we'll come out again. I bet his farm is near Lillian's."

"It's likely. There aren't that many farms on the island." Mildred sighed as she got back in the car. "It feels like we get close just to hit a roadblock."

"We'll get there." Priscilla thought of the other mysteries and puzzles that had fallen into her lap since moving to Martha's Vineyard and how they'd all been solved even when finding the answers seemed impossible.

"But we have to talk to Bowen to know what's really going on. Where could he be?" She sighed. "We could call the hotels on the island and see if they'll tell us whether he's a guest."

"Yes." Priscilla paused as something tickled at the edges of her mind.

"What is it?"

"There are so many hotels on the island, but I think I saw a note on Elmer's notepad. What was it?" She scrunched her eyes closed as she tried to remember what she had seen. "There were numbers, I can't remember those. But there were also words."

"You think they're important."

"Maybe." She thought a moment more. "I think there might have been a cabin involved."

"So it could reference a hotel or B&B."

"Possibly. Could you list those you can think of?"

Mildred started listing a bunch of hotels then paused. "The B&Bs don't have many guests, but there are quite a few around there. There's the Nobnocket Boutique Inn, the Hanover House, and Ashley Inn." She stopped, but Priscilla shrugged, so she kept going. "How about the Captain's Cabin?"

"Wait." Priscilla ran the words over in her mind and matched them up with the words on the paper. "I'm certain that's it."

"Perfect! That's just down the road." Mildred clicked her seat belt and turned to Priscilla. "What are you waiting for? Let's go."

The Captain's Cabin was a rustic-looking, oversized log cabin set in a grove of trees. Two rocking chairs sat abandoned on the long front porch, a pot of brittle mums sitting by the front door. Priscilla parked her car, and the women got out and walked up the sidewalk. As they approached the front door, it opened and a middle-aged man who carried some extra weight around his belly and a satchel over his shoulder stepped outside.

"That has to be him," Mildred mumbled. She raised her voice. "Bowen Thorton?"

The man's head jerked up, and he froze. His eyes widened, and he grasped his bag's strap and hurried to the sidewalk.

"Mr. Thorton, we just want to ask you a couple of questions." Priscilla stepped closer.

As she did, he dropped the satchel and took off running. While he was no Usain Bolt, he moved faster than either Priscilla or Mildred, and before they could reach him, he was in a blue sedan and flying down the long driveway.

"Do you think we should chase him?" Priscilla watched him turn right on the main road that led away from Vineyard Haven.

"I want to see what's in that satchel he dropped." Mildred marched over to the bag and carried it to the front porch. She sank onto one of the rockers and motioned for Priscilla to sit in the other. Then she unzipped the bag and gasped. "This has my documents."

CHAPTER TWENTY-FOUR

After her initial shock gave way to joy, Priscilla spoke. "I think we need to take that bag to the police, but first I want to see if anyone inside can tell us who that man was."

Mildred nodded. "I'll wait here."

The inside of the B&B was cozy, with hardwood floors and walls that were the exposed logs. Carpets lined the walkway to the front desk, with a table with coffee to the side. A few chairs were set in front of a large stone fireplace perfect for warming oneself on the cold nights that were coming. A young woman with a sleek ponytail stood behind the desk, wearing a navy suit. Her name tag read *Corrine*.

"Can I help you?"

"Did you see the man who left just a few minutes ago?"

"You mean Mr. Thorton?"

"Yes." Priscilla smiled. "I wondered if you could tell me how long he's been here."

"A couple of weeks now."

"Do you know how long he plans to stay?"

The young woman smiled at her with practiced detachment. "I really can't say."

"Of course. Thank you for your help." Priscilla went back out on the porch and headed to her car. "Come on, Mildred. I'll drop you at the police station so you can let them know that Bowen Thorton had your missing items."

"You're not coming in with me?"

"No, I have another stop to make." As soon as Mildred got out of her car at the police station, Priscilla drove to her house and retrieved the phone book. She paged through the thin volume until she came across the Jacksons. There were roughly forty Jacksons listed in the directory, and it didn't take long to find Shawn's number. She released a breath, grateful that he actually had a landline. She dialed his number and tapped her toes against the floor as she waited for either Shawn to pick up or the call to trip over to voice mail.

"Hello." The deep voice was friendly, if a bit distant.

"Hello, this is Priscilla Grant calling for Shawn Jackson."

"Speaking."

"I wondered if I might be able to come speak with you for a few minutes. I have some questions about the RMS *Republic*, and it seems you're quite the local expert."

"I am on certain things. Mind telling me specifically why you want to talk?" He released a short laugh. "I'd hate for you to drive all the way out here and be disappointed."

"It's no problem. I'm trying to track down some information. I saw your book the other day, and I think you would be the best person to speak with."

"Well, I'm happy to share what I can. Do you know how to get out here?"

"This is the address the phone book has for you." She rattled it off. "Is it correct?"

"Yep. It should take you about fifteen minutes from Vineyard Haven."

"Perfect. I'll be there in thirty. Thank you."

"No problem. I'll be here."

The question was, would Bowen be there too? She really wanted to be able to confront him in front of Shawn.

Next she called Mildred, who answered her cell. "Are you at the museum?"

"Just got back here. Figured the walk would do me good once the police didn't need me any longer."

"Is Carly still there?"

"Yes, the girl seems rooted to the spot."

"Great, because I'll be there in fifteen minutes to pick you up."

"Why? Where are we going?"

"To catch your thieves." She might not know the motivation exactly, but she was certain that Shawn could tell her why Bowen had the stolen items in his satchel. "Bring the satchel with you."

"I can't, since I took it to the police."

"That's right. Well, bring the list of missing items so we can confront Bowen with what he had."

"I'll be ready."

Fifteen minutes later when Priscilla pulled into the museum's parking lot, Mildred was waiting on the front porch, bundled up in her coat and scarf. As soon as she climbed into the SUV, she turned to Priscilla. "What did you learn?"

Priscilla quickly filled her in on her call to Shawn. "I'm not certain what he knows, but I don't think he's hiding anything. We'll find out for sure when we get to his place."

"If he's even there."

"I really think he will be. Besides, even if he is guilty, he doesn't know that the woman who called him just caught Bowen with the museum's property."

"I hope not." Mildred ran her fingers along the inside of the seat belt. "If he isn't there, I'm not sure what we'll do."

"We'll figure it out as we go. There's only so much we can plan out in detail." Priscilla understood the desire to reach the end of the puzzle and the fear that it would slip away from them. But she also knew it was out of their hands. All they could do was the best they could, and if that failed, try to convince Chief Hank Westin to take over.

The drive was picturesque, a part of the island that many visitors wouldn't see because it housed a few small farms and dairies. It was the same drive Priscilla had made several times that week when she helped Lillian get to town. She eased the car around a sharp curve and slowed even further as she noticed Al trying to steer a stray cow through a gate and back into a field.

"I think we're getting close." Priscilla glanced at her GPS. "This says we're only a little more than five miles from Shawn's home."

"I just hope we aren't too late." Mildred's voice held a weary note as she brushed her hands along both sides of her face.

Priscilla glanced at her then quickly returned her gaze to the road. "We'll know in a few minutes. Hang in there."

"It's just been a very long week. I had no idea when I agreed to host Deanie's birthday party that so much would happen as a result."

"Some of it has been good. If the medal hadn't disappeared, you might not have noticed that the other items were taken and known to look for them."

"But you did that work."

"Actually, Carly did a lot of it too."

"That's true." Mildred sighed. "I really misjudged her, and for that I'm sorry. Do you think she'd be interested in a job if I could afford to offer her one?"

"I don't know." But Priscilla really liked the idea. "I think she might have to finish school first."

"You're probably right, but I may feel her out."

Priscilla couldn't hide her smile at such a dramatic turnaround. "I'm glad you've resolved things with her."

"It's a start."

"Yes." Priscilla's foot crept to the brake as a car came hurtling toward them at a speed much too fast for the twisty, narrow road. "What on earth?"

"I think the driver is Bowen Thorton." Mildred's voice was shrill. "I knew he was going to get away."

Priscilla had to keep her focus on the road as she tried to watch the driver. As he inched farther over the middle line, she swerved to the right to keep from being hit. Her car bumped into the ditch, and an instant later, Bowen and his car flashed past.

"We have to stop him," Mildred screeched.

"Are you all right?"

"Not if he's getting away!"

"All right. Give me a minute." Priscilla dug her phone out and quickly placed a call. "Lillian, tell Al to open the gates and let the cows out."

"What?"

"I need him to create a barrier across the road. Quickly. I'll explain when I get there. Please? Can you trust me?"

Lillian hesitated just an instant. "All right, Priscilla. I hope you know what you're asking because most want us to keep the cows firmly within the fence."

"Thanks." Priscilla quickly hung up and then dialed the police. "Hello, this is Priscilla Grant. I've been pushed off the road by a reckless driver." She gave her approximate location and then answered a couple of questions. "We're fine, but if you could, would you send Officer April Brown out? She's been working with us on a matter tied to this accident. Thank you."

Mildred slowly turned to her, her eyes dulled. "What do we do now? Bowen surely got away."

"Maybe not. Al was right at the road with a cow. If he got my request, he could have let her back on the road without much effort."

"I suppose, but I really hope if he did, Bowen didn't hit her."

"No way he would be willing do that. While it would likely kill the cow, it would definitely total his car and probably injure him. I'm pretty certain he wouldn't be willing to risk that." She only hoped Lillian had time to get the message to Al, and he'd been willing to go along with her odd request. It was a lot to ask of new friends, but what else could she do? They weren't going anywhere while her car was stuck in the ditch.

She felt a bruise forming along her chest where the seat belt had restrained her. Fortunately, they'd hit the ditch at a slow enough speed that the airbags hadn't deployed. If she were really fortunate, then all she'd need is a tow and her car would be drivable again. "Do you think you're okay to get out of the car, or should I call for an ambulance?"

Mildred snorted, letting Priscilla know her friend's spirits would be fine. "It would take more than this to get me down."

Priscilla eased her neck in a gentle roll. "Let's be careful getting out. I have a feeling we may have some aches and bruises." And she was glad that was all. The way Bowen had barreled toward them, he hadn't been concerned about them and their safety.

They were fortunate to be so unscathed. But as a pickup truck eased in front of them, she noticed the driver was Shawn Jackson. She recognized his photo from the book. She just hoped he hadn't been sent by Bowen to finish the job.

CHAPTER TWENTY-FIVE

Shawn Jackson stepped from his battered pickup, a frown on his face, but Priscilla couldn't discern whether it was a frown of concern to find them on the side of the road or unhappiness that they were near his home. He strode toward her car, and Priscilla was grateful she hadn't exited yet.

He crouched to look through the window. "You ladies all right?"

"I think so." Priscilla eased in a breath. "I've already called the police, so hopefully they will be here soon."

"I don't like the idea of you waiting out here by yourself. It's fairly isolated, and if the police know you weren't injured, it might take them a while to get out here." He glanced back at his pickup that was still running on the side of the road. "How about I give you a ride?"

Priscilla exchanged a glance with Mildred. Would it be safe to get in his vehicle? She hoped so because she wasn't fond of the idea of staying on the side of the road. He was right. It could take the police a while to arrive.

Mildred didn't meet her gaze, but she did open her car door and ease out with a groan. "That'll leave a mark."

Shawn held up his hands and took a step back. "Ladies, I'm not sure what happened, but if it was a car driving too fast, I have a feeling it was driven by my brother. So sorry about that."

"If it was your brother, he was certainly reckless." Priscilla jutted her jaw as she exited the car, still uncertain whether she trusted Shawn.

"He was pretty mad at me when he left. When that happens, he tends to get a little emotional with his driving."

"That doesn't excuse driving us off the road." Mildred's voice was as stiff as her back.

"I agree, but you need to understand that he would never intentionally hurt you." He glanced from one to the other. "Neither would I. Let me help get you somewhere warm and safe to wait."

Mildred finally met Priscilla's gaze and gave a small nod.

"All right," Priscilla said. "You can drive us to the farm down the road."

"You mean the Salisburys' place?"

"Yes." Priscilla leaned back into her car to grab her purse and phone. "Do you need anything from in here, Mildred?"

"I didn't bring anything with me."

"Okay." She turned to Shawn and gave him her best intimidating stare. "We'll go a few miles with you."

"Yes, ma'am." He seemed amused by her attitude rather than cowed.

Priscilla sighed and hoped that at least his brother had been stopped by some cattle in the middle of the road. A minute later he helped Mildred and then Priscilla into the cab of his truck then walked around the vehicle and climbed behind the wheel.

Might as well ask him the questions that brought us here. "So you're the local expert on the RMS *Republic*."

He nodded but didn't so much as look at her.

"Can you tell me why you're interested in it?"

"Because I like the idea of finding the treasure. Every little boy dreams of pirates and gold. We have this shipwreck right off our coast, and it captured my attention." He shrugged. "I thought it would be easy to do, but even now that I have the salvage rights, it's elusive. That's what had Bowen all out of sorts. I've borrowed money from him for years to fund the dream."

"That's nice of him."

"Yeah, but he got tired of waiting. Thought if he came to see me this summer he could persuade me to try to find another local ship-wreck he was researching. He said that even though others couldn't find it, he had some ideas about how to locate its position on the ocean floor. Unfortunately, whatever information he thought he had didn't help all that much."

"What do you mean?"

"I'm not exactly sure what he was talking about. I told him I couldn't conduct a search based on incomplete data. He tried to get me to believe he would eventually come up with the exact coordinates, but I can't afford guesswork."

"Do you have investors?"

"Not enough. Most of them are weary and disillusioned. Bowen thought he could add the *oomph* to get it done." Shawn gave a wry chuckle. "He was wrong."

"I'm sorry."

"It's the way of these things. The winner is often the most tenacious person." He slowed as the road curved. "He came to the house just after you called and admitted to me that he'd gotten his information about the *Liverpool* from documents and maps and a journal, all stolen from the museum. He got angry when I refused to even look at the artifacts, and that's when he took off down the road. I followed him and found you in the ditch."

Priscilla felt her nerves ease as she spotted the cluster of trees and barn that marked the Salisburys' farm. "Well, when we catch up with Bowen, we can ask if it was worth it."

Shawn chuckled as he slowed for a final curve. "I doubt he'll think it was." He pushed hard on the brakes. "What on earth?"

Mildred clapped her hands together. "Your crazy idea worked, Priscilla."

Priscilla looked through the windshield and started laughing. Bowen's sedan was surrounded by a bunch of cows, and he stomped around his vehicle, gesturing wildly. Al Salisbury just watched, a grin on his face as he did nothing to move the cattle. Lillian leaned on his arm and seemed to be saying something to Bowen, but the man didn't even slow down as he continued to pace circles around his car.

Then on the other side of the logjam, a police cruiser crested a hill with lights flashing. Bowen slumped as he looked from the cows to the cruiser back to his brother's pickup. Shawn parked his truck in the middle of the road, and the cruiser pulled to a stop. A minute later Chief Westin stepped from one side while Officer Brown stepped from the other. The cows seemed entranced by the swirling lights, and Bowen didn't bother to try to get away.

Chief Westin worked his way through the cows to Al. "Can you tell me what's going on?"

Al shook his head with a grin. "Lillian got a call from Priscilla asking us to let the cows out. I opened the gate and shooed the first one through when this guy comes up over the hill. He was smart enough to stop, just in time to let some more of the girls come find his car."

Chief Westin looked at Priscilla. "Mrs. Grant, do you have a good reason for asking this man to let his cows out? I'll deal with his judgment on actually doing it later."

"This man, Bowen Thorton, ran us off the road a few miles back, and we have good reason to believe he's the one who's been taking items from the East Shore Historical Museum archives." She met the chief's gaze, knowing this had been about their only option to slow Bowen down. "I didn't want him to get away before we could talk to him. I also knew a smart man would stop before plowing into a fifteen-hundred-pound cow."

"Is that so?" Chief Westin shook his head. "You're just lucky he saw the cow in time to stop. Otherwise, you might have a claim against you for destruction of property."

Priscilla swallowed, hard. "Then I'm glad it all worked out."

"Me too." She could tell he was fighting a smile by the way the edges of his mouth twitched. Then he turned to Bowen. "This should be real interesting," he said.

The man looked around as if trying to find a way of escape, but from his arms-crossed brother on one side, to the cows, to the police on the other side, he was trapped and he knew it. He slumped against his car as one of the milk cows strolled toward him. When her hoof came within inches of his foot, he blanched. "Could we please get the cows back where they belong?"

"Sure," Al drawled. "Just as soon as you answer whatever questions Priscilla has."

She nodded her thanks to him. "I just want to know if you are indeed the person who has been taking the maps, diaries, and other papers from the museum archives."

His face drooped. "I am."

"You were looking for information about the *Liverpool*, weren't you?"

Bowen's jaw dropped. "How do you know about the *Liverpool*?" he demanded. "Have there been other treasure seekers coming to the museum and asking about it?"

Chief Westin frowned at him. "You mean to tell me there's another shipwreck around here besides the *Republic*?"

"I mean exactly that," Bowen said. "Everyone's been so focused on the *Republic* that they've ignored rumors of similar transport on the *Liverpool*." Excitement laced his voice as he continued. "The *Liverpool* went down in better water and with a cargo of riches on it. If we can actually recover those, it's worth more than the wealth of the *Republic* that is destined to stay on the bottom of the ocean."

Chief Westin looked at Mildred. "Do you want to press charges?"

"Yes, I think I do." She glanced at Priscilla. "I at least want him to think hard before he does something like this again. I also want to know if he has any more records from the archives."

Bowen hung his head. "I have a few more files that you didn't get earlier today. I was going to photocopy them and then return them."

Mildred shrieked and stood tall. "Do you not understand how much damage a photocopy machine can do to old documents?"

"I know how to be careful."

"Well, I'm still glad we got you before you could do that. Those are irreplaceable files."

"Then you should start treating them that way. It was way too easy to walk off with them." The challenge was clear.

"I will. Carly and I are working on it even now."

"Good." Bowen addressed Chief Westin. "Want me to come in with you?"

"I think that would be best." The chief turned to Al. "Can he leave his car here?"

"Sure."

"Need any help corralling these cattle?" Merriment danced in the chief's eyes. "I cannot believe you actually went along with the harebrained idea to use them to block the road."

"It may not be the smartest thing I've done, but it worked."

Twenty minutes later the last cow was herded back inside the fence. Priscilla walked over to join Al and Lillian at the gate. "Thank you so much for your help."

"I'm just glad it ended well." Lillian smiled at her. "While it was an odd request, you've helped me so much, it seemed the least we could do was try to help you back."

Al nodded. "I'd just gotten Dolly back to the gate, so it was easy enough to shoo her back out to the road. I'm just glad the driver had the good sense to stop."

"Me too." The alternative made Priscilla a little nauseous. "I hope you both will join me for Thanksgiving dinner."

"We'd love to." Lillian smiled at her. "I'll bring a sweet potato casserole and anything else you need."

"Perfect." Mildred cleared her throat, and Priscilla knew it was time to go. "Thanks again."

Lillian stopped her. "I had an idea. What do you think about me painting Deanie in her WASP uniform? We could have a copy for the museum."

"I love that idea. You could even add images of her WASP colleagues."

"Definitely. If you think it's a good idea, I'll call her in the morning."

"I think she'll be thrilled. What do you think, Mildred?"

"I like the idea of something like that at the museum to go with her display. Speaking of the museum, I really need to get back. I'm feeling foolish standing here in my 1790s outfit in the middle of the road." Mildred plucked at her long skirt.

Priscilla gave her friends a hug then glanced at Shawn. "Willing to drive us to town?"

"Least I can do. I'll also make sure a tow truck gets out here today."

"Thank you. I really need my car to get around."

Twenty minutes later he dropped them off at the museum. It didn't take long to update Carly, who was thrilled as she flipped through the items Bowen had given them.

She finished looking through the stack. "I think almost everything is back."

"Bowen said he would return the remaining items to us." Mildred relaxed into the chair behind the registration desk. "It's such a relief to have this be over. And I love the ideas you have for enhancing security. We could make a good team."

Carly's cheeks colored. "Maybe, but first I have to finish my bachelor's degree. It'll be back to college for me in January. After I wrap up the semester, we can talk."

"Agreed."

An hour later, a tow truck dropped Priscilla's car off. The man behind the wheel assured her the vehicle was fine and ready to drive. As she drove home, Priscilla allowed herself to bask in the good feelings of another puzzle solved and another friend helped.

CHAPTER TWENTY-SIX

Thanksgiving morning dawned with a frosted sky that threatened to hide the sun. Priscilla got up early to get the turkey in the oven then took a quick stroll along the shore with Jake. Then it was time to settle into preparations for the Thanksgiving meal. A day she'd dreaded when Rachel had told her it was too short of a time to visit had now turned into a day of anticipation.

Her community on the island was growing. Carly, Lillian and Al, and Joan were coming for dinner. She'd been surprised when Joan had accepted her invitation, but her cousin had assured her that her boys had decided to go on an adventure together. She'd been thrilled to have somewhere to go and people she loved to spend the holiday with.

As Priscilla set the place mats and napkins around the table, she smiled at the centerpiece. It was a cornucopia filled with fall flowers that Mildred had sent. Priscilla understood that it was Mildred's way of saying thanks, and she quickly checked the florist's sponge to make sure the flowers still had water. The bouquet was too pretty to let die from lack of attention.

An hour later at noon, her friends arrived. Carly looked relaxed and young, as if solving the mystery and having her fears laid to rest had allowed her to let the stress go. Then Lillian and Al arrived,

Lillian without any crutches. "As long as I take it easy, the doctor said I don't need to use those horrible things."

"That's wonderful news." Priscilla took Lillian's and Al's coats and hung them on the coat tree. "I bet you're delighted to have more freedom. Just don't overdo it."

"Al is making sure I'm careful. It's easy to want to do too much now that I'm free."

Joan arrived with the rolls and an apple pie. After Priscilla introduced her to everyone, Joan asked, "Do you need any help, or are we ready to sit down to a bounty of food?"

"We'll eat just as soon as I bring the food out."

Lillian noted her setting aside small portions on a paper plate. "What's that for?"

"Deanie isn't able to join us, but Andrew is going to swing by and get a plate for her."

"Why don't I make one for him too?"

"Perfect. It's something I should have thought to do."

In no time the plates were ready and covered with foil, and then everyone gathered around Priscilla's table that was overloaded with so much food, she didn't know how they'd eat it all.

Happy conversation was flowing when someone knocked at the door.

"That must be Andrew. Keep eating, this'll just take a moment." Priscilla quickly stood and got to the door. When she opened it, Gerald stood there in his Coast Guard uniform and heavy pea coat. "Gerald. What a surprise. Please come in!"

"Thanks, but I'm working."

"Oh, then let me prepare a plate you can take with you. You can have some Thanksgiving while you work."

"That would be nice, but before you do that, I stopped by to let you know Jake got out."

Priscilla glanced back and noticed that Jake wasn't under the table, his normal haunt when food was out. "Jake? Here, boy." When only silence met her call, she sighed. "You must be right. Let me grab my coat, his leash, and a treat. Hopefully we can entice him inside quickly."

"It might take more than a treat. When I last saw him, he was happily chasing seagulls on the beach."

Al walked up and handed her a napkin. "I bet this turkey will do the trick."

"I hate to spoil him for sneaking away, but I want to eat while the food's still warm." Priscilla pulled on her coat and accepted the turkey. "Thank you."

Gerald held the door for her, and she followed him along the path to the shore.

"So the Coast Guard works on Thanksgiving?"

"Every day." He walked alongside her by the water, his hands clasped behind his back.

As she glanced at him through the corner of her eye, she noted again how handsome he looked in his uniform. "Well, I'm glad you were on the job to let me know about Jake. That silly pup doesn't understand how great he has it at the cottage."

"Someday he will." Gerald stopped and pointed across a short dune. "There he is."

The silly dog's tongue was lolling out of his mouth as he chased one seagull only to be distracted by another.

"Jake. Come here, boy." His head turned at her words, and she held up the napkin. "Look, boy. It's a treat."

He gave one last half-hearted lunge at a seagull then loped toward her, a happy smile on his face. She snapped the leash on his collar and gave him the turkey. Slowly she and Gerald walked back to the cottage where her friends waited. "Are you sure you won't come in for a quick bite? I understand that you can't stay, but surely you get a break."

Gerald faced her and studied her so long that heat began to climb her neck. "I'd like that."

A few minutes later, Jake slumbered at her side, and Gerald had joined the group at the table. As Priscilla glanced around at her friends, she thanked God for bringing her to Martha's Vineyard at the time when she needed these new friends and family so much. Her heart was truly full as she eagerly looked to the future.

AUTHOR LETTER

Dear Reader,

In *Making Waves*, Priscilla is wrestling with some hard realities in life. While Martha's Vineyard is beginning to feel like home, Priscilla is still in the throes of finding community. I will never forget when my husband, Eric, and I left DC so he could take a job in small-town Indiana. It was a homecoming for him, but it was all new and lonely and overwhelming for me. I went from a full-time job that I loved, with a career trajectory, to being lost and isolated.

It was a hard season.

But as I look back now, I can see God's hand in that move. I clung to the truth that because we were a unit, if God had a place for Eric—which was so abundantly clear—then He had a place for me. I just had to trust Him and do my part to find it.

It was in Indiana that I met Colleen Coble and my writing dreams took off. It was in Indiana that I began teaching and slowly advanced to a full-time teaching career at a Big Ten university. It was in Indiana that I found a church where I could serve and minister as my heart longed to do. And it was in Indiana that I found a law firm that let me practice as little or as much as I like.

Wherever you are, whether it's in the midst of a move, still feeling isolated after a move, or in the embrace of real community, know it is possible. God will bring people into your life that can become your heart sisters. Trust Him and look around with expectation.

Enjoy!

Cara Putman

ABOUT THE AUTHORS

Tricia Goyer is a busy mom of ten, grandmother of two, and wife to John. Somewhere around the hustle and bustle of family life, she manages to find the time to write fictional tales delighting and entertaining readers and nonfiction titles offering encouragement and hope. A best-selling author, Tricia has published more than sixty books to date and has written more than five hundred articles. She is a two-time Carol Award winner, as well as a Christy and ECPA Award nominee. In addition to her roles as mom, wife, and author, Tricia volunteers around her community and mentors teen moms. She is the founder of Hope Pregnancy Ministries in Northwestern Montana, and she currently leads a Teen MOPS Group in Little Rock, AR. Learn more about Tricia at triciagoyer.com.

Cara Putman is an award-winning author of more than twenty-five novels, doing what she dreamed of as a teenager. She loves watching the movie in her head and transcribing it for readers. In her spare time she homeschools her children, teaches at Purdue University, and serves on the board of American Christian Fiction Writers. You can learn more about Cara at caraputman .com. Be sure to find her on Facebook, Instagram, and Twitter. She loves connecting with readers!

AN ARMCHAIR TOUR OF MARTHA'S VINEYARD

Vineyard Haven WASPs

Because Tricia and I both have written numerous World War II novels, it's not unusual to find a World War II connection in our contemporary novels like *Making Waves*. You may have wondered if Deanie was a real person. She's a figment of our imaginations but based on real-life heroes like Ann Lesnikowski. During World War II, Ann served as a Women's Airforce Service Pilot (WASP) until the service was ended in 1944. It wasn't until 2010, when she was ninety-five, that her service along with that of the other WASPs was recognized with the Congressional Gold Medal.

It was also interesting to learn that the founder of the WASPs was another Vineyard Haven resident, Nancy Harkness Love. These women freed men to serve overseas by flying solo, delivering to places from factory plants to airbases. It wasn't until 1977 that the women who served as WASPs were afforded veteran status with its benefits. And it wasn't until 2010 that the public at large began to understand their service through the recognition that the Congressional Gold Medal brought.

When asked about her fondest memories of her time serving, Ann emphasized the companionship among the women. What a wonderful group to honor through our character Deanie, and Deanie was the perfect character to help Priscilla learn about friendship.

SOMETHING DELICIOUS FROM OUR SEASIDE FRIENDS

Cinnamon Scones
from Candy Lane Confectionery
(You can't eat just one!)

Scones

2¼ cups all-purpose flour

1 teaspoon salt

1½ teaspoons baking powder

½ teaspoon baking soda

½ cup white sugar

2 teaspoons cinnamon

½ cup (1 stick) cold butter, cut in cubes

1 cup sour milk or sour half-and-half (you can "sour" milk by adding 2 tablespoons vinegar per cup)

Topping

1 egg, well-beaten

½ cup cinnamon-sugar mixture (about 5/1 sugar/cinnamon)

Icing

1 cup powdered sugar

2 tablespoons butter, softened

2 tablespoons half-and-half or liquid coffee creamer

1 teaspoon vanilla

Scones: Sift together flour, salt, baking powder, baking soda, sugar, and cinnamon. "Cut" the butter into the dry ingredients with a pastry cutter until the mixture is like fine bread crumbs. Add the sour milk. Stir quickly with a fork until the dough forms a ball.

Dust your hands with flour and turn the dough onto a floured board. Knead gently about ten times, working in a small amount of additional flour. Flatten the dough into a one-inch thick circle. (It will be twelve to fifteen inches in diameter.)

"Paint" the circle of dough with the beaten egg (depending on the size of the egg, it may only take half of the mixture). Then sprinkle the cinnamon-sugar mixture evenly over the top of the dough circle.

Using a pizza cutter or sharp knife, slice the dough pizza-style into twelve equal triangles. Transfer to a greased cookie sheet, leaving a half-inch between scones. Bake for twelve to fifteen minutes in a preheated 425-degree oven. Scones are done when they have a light golden color.

Icing: Mix the ingredients together in a bowl. When thoroughly mixed, slather the icing on top of each scone. Enjoy!

Read on for a sneak peek of another exciting book
in the series Mysteries of Martha's Vineyard!

Don't Rock the Boat
by Elizabeth Ludwig

Priscilla Latham Grant tugged her collar tight around her ears and let the brisk December wind whipping off the Atlantic sweep across her icy cheeks. She smiled as she inhaled deeply of the salt-scented air. There was something so invigorating about these early morning walks, something so encouraging and joyful. Even with scattered cloud cover, it promised to be a glorious day.

Giving the zipper on her coat one last snug under her chin, she set off. The sand gave beneath her feet with every step, making her daily walk more vigorous than normal, but she enjoyed the feeling of straining toward something. Today, the goal was a secluded cove just around the bend from her lighthouse.

Ahead of her, Jake romped in the light dusting of snow that capped the sand and dunes. When he tired of that, he dashed into the frigid waves, chasing a fish or perhaps a scrap of seaweed. Priscilla groaned and curled her fingers inside her mittens. The dog would need a bath after this walk was over.

"Jake, come back." He ignored her and zipped into a mound of swaying beach grass. She cupped one hand to her mouth and called again over the crashing waves. "Jake!"

His twitching tail said he heard but wasn't quite inclined to obey. He lifted his head and then he stiffened, his tail going from twitching to ramrod straight.

Priscilla frowned. The dog was below her, near the shore. She picked her way down the hill toward him, mindful that the sand could easily give way and send her tumbling. "Jake, what are you looking at?"

He barked once and then began an incessant yapping that grew louder as she picked up her pace. Her calves complained as her booted feet dug into the sand. Granted, she took these walks for exercise, but her muscles were surely going to complain tomorrow.

"What is it, boy?" Priscilla struggled for breath against the sharp bite of the wind. "What do you see?"

Jake's furry head turned toward her, and his warm chocolate eyes begged her to come and look.

Priscilla reached for his collar and tugged him back from something half-buried in the sand. "What is that?"

Jake whimpered and clawed at the sand.

"Stop, Jake," Priscilla commanded. She nudged him aside with her foot and bent for a closer look. Hints of brown peeked through the clumps of seaweed and sand. She also thought she glimpsed the sheen of metal. A clasp of some sort?

Curling her lip in disgust, she reached down with two fingers and pulled the seaweed back, exposing bits of tattered leather.

"A briefcase?"

She looked at Jake, who tipped his head to stare at her curiously. If he could talk, he surely would have asked, "What's a briefcase?"

Priscilla shrugged and dropped down to her knees in the cold sand. With fingers curled inside her mittens, she scraped back enough of the sand to see that the object was much larger than a briefcase.

"It's a suitcase."

She turned, but Jake appeared to have lost interest in the discovery and was nipping at the seaweed she'd pushed aside. Ugh. Now he'd smell of wet sand *and* fish. She'd be lucky to get the smell out of his fur with two baths.

Bending back to her task, Priscilla continued digging until she had most of the suitcase exposed. A couple of tugs on the handle, and it slid free. Despite the scratches marring the surface, she could tell the suitcase was good quality. Leather straps with brass buckles protected each end, and there was a brass lock below the handle for added security. Priscilla eyed it curiously. How had a suitcase that appeared to be in relatively good condition ended up on her beach?

A foghorn sounded, and Priscilla looked up to see a gleaming ship chugging toward shore. Judging by its size, it would probably end up in Boston Harbor. Priscilla glanced back at the suitcase. Plenty of ships sailed past her beach and the Misty Harbor Lighthouse left to her by her aunt, Marjorie Latham, and that wasn't even counting the ones that ferried tourists from the mainland every day. This old suitcase could have come from any one of them. Or worse . . . a boat could have capsized.

Concern gripped her stomach as she looked both ways up the beach. She hated to think of a person struggling in the frigid waters of the Atlantic. This time of year, it wouldn't take them long to succumb to hypothermia, and that was assuming they could fight their way through the pounding waves.

Fortunately, only rippling sand and swaying grass stretched along the shore. Priscilla breathed a relieved sigh and then tipped the suitcase upright and gave it a shake. It didn't feel empty. She stood and picked it up by the handle. It was heavy, but that could be simply because it was waterlogged. The only way to know for sure would be to drag it back to the cottage and pry open the lock.

"Jake!"

This time when she called, he bounded to her side, his fur wet and matted with sand.

"You know you're not coming into the house like that, right?" she scolded.

Oblivious to his bedraggled condition, Jake yipped happily and ran on ahead. Tipping the suitcase onto one edge, Priscilla half-dragged, half-carried it up the beach toward her cottage. Too bad it didn't have wheels like its more modern counterparts, not that wheels would have helped much in the sand, she realized as she bumped it up the stairs onto her porch. Pausing to catch her breath, she swiped the back of her hand over her brow and rested her hip against the side of the cottage. Walks on the beach were one thing, but what she'd just done amounted to a full-fledged workout.

She took off her mittens and studied her raw hands. Blisters were already forming on her palms. Maybe later she could swing by Candy Lane's bakery and indulge in a couple of chocolate chip cookies as a reward for having worked so hard. But first...

She bent and clasped the handle, bumping and dragging the suitcase inside until it rested fully on her kitchen table. She grimaced at the trail of sand left in her wake. She'd only dragged in half the beach with her. Jake gave himself a shake and deposited the other half onto the floor.

"Jake, no!"

She sighed as he trotted off toward the living room. She'd have to sweep up the mess later. Right now, she was dying for a peek inside that suitcase. She paused. Except...

Maybe she should examine it first and see if she could figure out who it belonged to before breaking open the lock. Though she longed to give in to her curiosity, practicality won out. She slid out of her coat then grabbed a damp cloth and began wiping away the sand and grit that remained while she looked for initials or a luggage tag. When she didn't find any, she bit her lip and bent to examine the lock.

A warm, furry body bumped against her legs, and she glanced down to see that Jake had returned, his ears perked and his head tilted to one side as he looked at her.

"What?" Priscilla shooed him with the towel. "It's your fault we even have the suitcase. After all, you're the one who found it."

Jake settled to the floor with a moan, his head resting glumly against his paws.

Priscilla smiled. Having Jake around was like having a live-in friend. She talked to him like a real person, and sometimes she was certain he understood.

Leaning down, Priscilla examined the suitcase closely. The lock was the old-fashioned variety—the kind that needed a key to open. She gave it a jiggle and a few grains of wet sand spattered onto the table.

"Great. More sand." She gave the suitcase another jiggle. "Well, Jake, I certainly won't be able to get this lock open until I get all the sand out."

Sometimes she thought he understood. This was not one of those times.

Sighing, Priscilla crossed to her cupboards, pulled out a drawer, and rummaged until she found a basting brush.

"Perfect."

She scooped up the brush and set about clearing away as much of the sand as she could from the lock. When that was done, she went back to the drawer and removed a small paring knife. Though it was slim, the blade was still too thick to fit in the lock. She set the knife aside and frowned. Now what?

Her gaze settled on a grill fork. She lifted an eyebrow. Before he died, her husband Gary had teased her a time or two about her makeshift tools—butter knives instead of screwdrivers and heeled shoes instead of hammers—but this was one instance where she was glad for her unique way of viewing the items in her cupboards and closets.

She carried the two-tined fork to the suitcase. After a little finagling, she realized the long, slender tines would certainly fit in the lock, but she would have to bend one of them out of the way if she wanted to slide the other inside.

She went back to the cupboard, but this time she came back with a pair of pliers she kept handy and made short work of the second tine on the grill fork. As she'd thought, the remaining tine slid easily into the lock, but it was only with a little coaxing from the flat side of the pliers that she was finally able to force the thing open.

At the satisfying click, Jake lifted his head and peered up at her. Priscilla rested her hand against the top of the suitcase and met his gaze.

"Well? Are we sure we want to know what's inside?"

He gave a soft whimper.

"I'm curious too, but what if we don't like what we find?"

Jake yawned, as if to say, "What could possibly be so bad?"

"Right." She sucked in a breath. "Here goes nothing."

Though she wanted to look, Priscilla's heart beat a peculiar rhythm as she reached for the handle. This suitcase belonged to someone once. What if that person lost their life in the Atlantic? Would they really want her riffling through their things? She shuddered at the morbid thought. On the other hand, how would she ever know who the suitcase belonged to if she didn't look inside? Obviously, she wouldn't.

The argument settled, she took a deep breath, counted to three, and then slowly lifted the lid.

A NOTE FROM THE EDITORS

We hope you enjoyed Mysteries of Martha's Vineyard, published by the Books and Inspirational Media Division of Guideposts, a nonprofit organization that touches millions of lives every day through products and services that inspire, encourage, help you grow in your faith, and celebrate God's love.

Thank you for making a difference with your purchase of this book, which helps fund our many outreach programs to military personnel, prisons, hospitals, nursing homes, and educational institutions.

We also create many useful and uplifting online resources. Visit Guideposts.org to read true stories of hope and inspiration, access OurPrayer network, sign up for free newsletters, download free e-books, join our Facebook community, and follow our stimulating blogs.

To learn about other Guideposts publications, including the best-selling devotional *Daily Guideposts*, go to Guideposts.org/Shop, call (800) 932-2145, or write to Guideposts, PO Box 5815, Harlan, Iowa 51593.

Sign up for the Guideposts Fiction Newsletter
and stay up-to-date on the books you love!

You'll get sneak peeks of new releases, recommendations from other Guideposts readers, and special offers just for you . . .

and it's FREE!

Just go to Guideposts.org/Newsletters today to sign up.

Guideposts.

Visit Guideposts.org/Shop
or call (800) 932-2145

Find more inspiring fiction in these best-loved Guideposts series!

Mysteries of Martha's Vineyard

Come to the shores of this quaint and historic island and dig in to a cozy mystery. When a recent widow inherits a lighthouse just off the coast of Massachusetts, she finds exciting adventures, new friends, and renewed hope.

Tearoom Mysteries

Mix one stately Victorian home, a charming lakeside town in Maine, and two adventurous cousins with a passion for tea and hospitality. Add a large scoop of intriguing mystery and sprinkle generously with faith, family, and friends, and you have the recipe for Tearoom Mysteries.

Sugarcreek Amish Mysteries

Be intrigued by the suspense and joyful "aha!" moments in these delightful stories. Each book in the series brings together two women of vastly different backgrounds and traditions, who realize there's much more to the "simple life" than meets the eye.

Mysteries of Silver Peak

Escape to the historic mining town of Silver Peak, Colorado, and discover how one woman's love of antiques helps her solve mysteries buried deep in the town's checkered past.

Patchwork Mysteries

Discover that life's little mysteries often have a common thread in a series where every novel contains an intriguing whodunit centered around a quilt located in a beautiful New England town.

To learn more about these books, visit Guideposts.org/Shop